PENGUIN BOOKS

THE HABIT OF LOVE

Namita Gokhale is a writer, publisher and co-director of the Jaipur Literature Festival. Her books include the novels *Priya: In Incredible Indyaa*, *A Himalayan Love Story*, *Gods, Graves and Grandmother*, *The Book of Shadows*, *Shakuntala: The Play of Memory* and *Paro*, and the non-fiction works *The Book of Shiva* and *Mountain Echoes: Reminiscences of Kumaoni Women*. She has also retold the Mahabharata for young readers and co-edited *In Search of Sita: Revisiting Mythology* with Dr Malashri Lal.

The Habit of Love

Namita Gokhale

PENGUIN BOOKS

PENGUIN BOOKS
Published by the Penguin Group
Penguin Books India Pvt. Ltd, 11 Community Centre, Panchsheel Park, New Delhi 110 017, India
Penguin Group (USA) Inc., 375 Hudson Street, New York, New York 10014, USA
Penguin Group (Canada), 90 Eglinton Avenue East, Suite 700, Toronto, Ontario, M4P 2Y3, Canada (a division of Pearson Penguin Canada Inc.)
Penguin Books Ltd, 80 Strand, London WC2R 0RL, England
Penguin Ireland, 25 St Stephen's Green, Dublin 2, Ireland (a division of Penguin Books Ltd)
Penguin Group (Australia), 250 Camberwell Road, Camberwell, Victoria 3124, Australia (a division of Pearson Australia Group Pty Ltd)
Penguin Group (NZ), 67 Apollo Drive, Rosedale, Auckland 0632, New Zealand (a division of Pearson New Zealand Ltd)
Penguin Group (South Africa) (Pty) Ltd, 24 Sturdee Avenue, Rosebank, Johannesburg 2196, South Africa

Penguin Books Ltd, Registered Offices: 80 Strand, London WC2R 0RL, England

First published by Penguin Books India 2012

Copyright © Namita Gokhale 2012

10 9 8 7 6 5 4 3 2

ISBN 9780143417729

For sale in the Indian Subcontinent only

Typeset in Sabon MT by Eleven Arts, Delhi
Printed at Sanat Printers, Kundli, Haryana

To my mother, Neerja Pant, for being an evolved listener of told and untold stories

Contents

Contents

Life on Mars

When I first saw Udit Narain, I recognized instantly that he was a crank. Because I am a crank myself, I can sniff out another aberrant personality. Our pheromones, our ganglia and our neurons wave out to each other. Since genuine cranks are normally shy, it usually ends there, but with Udit I found that we spent most of the cocktail hour at my best friend's crowded birthday party with each other. He was my friend's younger brother's friend, he was actually young enough to be my son.

I have three sons, they are scattered in colleges and universities around the world. They rarely write to me. They manage to send 'Wish you were here' kind of postcards without forwarding addresses and in incomprehensible handwriting. There are also birthday cards, always posted

3

a few months too early or too late. I have a suspicion that none of them really knows when my birthday is, but as in all likelihood they don't care, I take the cards in my stride, as I have taken my life since my husband died over a decade ago.

So I knew how to handle Udit, and I listened patiently as he told me about life on Mars. 'It brings our own lives back into perspective,' he said, in his gentle wheezy voice, 'when we realize that we're not the only life form in the universe.'

Now I don't care about life on Mars, I spend my energies on day-to-day survival, I hold a job and I freelance for a few papers, I have a part-time maid who never comes on time, and the water supply in my part of the town can be very erratic. There is little joy in my life, Delhi is an enervating city to live in, it is always too hot or too cold, and what with deadlines and press conferences and crowded parties which I always leave early, you could say that I'm very lonely and you would be right. Even seeing my name in print doesn't give me a lift anymore—Madhu Sinha in bold typeface at the bottom of the page. But a facial makes things look better, and so does a good dinner. Sometimes, when a few of us college friends get together, we let our hair down and put our feet up, and down a fair amount of rum and beer and forget for a while how awful life really is.

Udit's slightly asthmatic stutter made me feel protective. He was very different from my sons, who are all athletic, brilliant and heartless. I expect they'll marry tall blondes and settle down wherever the urge strikes them, but at no cost do I ever intend to arrange a marriage for them or anything like that. I had an arranged marriage myself, and it was a happy marriage. Then he took that fateful flight to Calcutta, and when he died a large part of me died as well. I know my sons carry a bit of that hurt with them still, wherever they are, and they worry about me and intend to look after me; it's just that they're young and unthinking and daily life takes its toll on them as it does on me.

Udit didn't bother about daily life at all, it was as though it didn't exist, he never noticed what he ate, he didn't lust after girls, and he wasn't worried about earning a living. I didn't know anything about his parents or his family. He would visit me every Thursday, a large ash tilak on his forehead, and I looked forward to his visit. I'm not a good cook but I'd stock his favourite brand of cigarettes and make him some coffee, and as he never ate anything, I never ventured beyond offering him imported biscuits from a fancy tin, which I usually ended up eating myself.

It wasn't only life on Mars that Udit would talk about. He talked about biodiversity and fuzzy logic and the poetry of Rilke and all kinds of non-specific things. He never talked about a job, I knew he didn't have one, but life on Mars is different from life in Delhi and how could I explain to Udit what it was like to bring up three children, three boys, and watch them grow up and turn their backs on me? For that's what it was, my sons had forgotten about me and abandoned me. When Udit came to see me on Thursday every week and bathed me in his unquestioning affection, I could see this quite clearly.

He borrowed money from me only once, a pitiable, negligible amount that even I could afford to lend, and returned it promptly the very next week. Mysteriously, he remembered my birthday, though I had never told him when it was, and he actually brought me a sari, a Kanjeevaram cotton in subtle earth colours. In short, he had become a part of my life and he assuaged my loneliness and made life bearable in the emotional desert that Delhi had become for me.

The day the report about the meteorite hit the papers—the one about the lump of rock that displayed biological activity—Udit quite naturally went mad. Mad with joy, mad with relief. 'I told you so,' he said, his voice alift with exhilaration. 'Didn't I always tell you? We are not alone!'

Then I was subjected to an hour of earnest analysis. He told me about the little lump of rock, all two kilos of it, and how it had been formed by volcanic activity four and a half billion years ago. He told me how it was blasted away from the mother planet by the impact of another asteroid, and how it had orbited the sun till some thirteen thousand years ago, when it landed on our lap right here in Antarctica.

'What a long journey,' I said indulgently, and made him another cup of coffee: the first one had gone cold with all the talk and a fly had drowned in it. Udit threw his cigarette butt into the coffee cup, which was a habit I detested but he was in such a good mood that I didn't say anything.

When I discovered that I had cancer it came as no surprise. I had sensed that things were happening to my body, my insides were sullen and stagnant and surging with latent anger, and then there were my fears, my very real fears, about money and old age and even about death. Yes, I was scared of dying. I wondered if my sons would finally turn up if I were to die, or if they would merely send consolatory postcards to each other across great distances. And my breasts—my large, well-suckled pendulous breasts on which these strapping monsters had once fed—were beginning to hurt. There was a lump in my right breast that never seemed to go away, and when I had the mammography, and the large redundant blob of flesh was pinioned inside the metallic holder, the doctor looked pained and sickened and said nothing. It was my gynaecologist who told me that I had breast cancer.

My three college friends, the ones with whom I used to drink rum, rushed to my aid. Before I knew it, I was in hospital, being wheeled around on a rattling trolley, well, not a trolley but a stretcher, and there were arc lights and men in green overalls wearing masks. As the anaesthesia got to me, I discovered that I was on Mars, there were masked men in green overalls everywhere, and life on Mars wasn't really so different from life in Delhi. It was difficult, tedious and painful. Then, suddenly, a strange white light flooded the room, and I felt a sense of power and control and expectation, as I felt myself leave that misused, malaise-ridden body and float out of its confined chaotic cell structure into the crowded corridor outside the operation theatre, quite oblivious to the visible consternation of the surgeon, Dr Patnaik, I think it was, his slim surgeon's hands in their sterile gloves flapping like dying fish. Outside in the corridor, the air was very still and nobody noticed me as I floated out of the corridor to the balcony.

I looked out and I saw the intersection between AIIMS and Safdarjung Hospital. The air was static with despair, and everywhere I could hear screams—loud screams, whispered screams, strangulated screams. I noticed that a single Reebok shoe was lying on a ledge beyond the balcony: a new shoe, sleek, expensive, inexplicable, ludicrous. I wondered what it was doing there, but then suddenly I was wrenched back by some powerful force, it was as though somebody had grabbed me by the shoulder and pulled me back. I was dragged away from the balcony and drawn back past the crowded corridor where the flies buzzed, through the closed doors back into the OT where Dr Patnaik was still in a tizzy.

When I awoke the next day in the hospital room (it was a room with two beds, but I was the only occupant), the first thing I saw was the bottle-green cloth screen that divided the room. I have always wondered why it's called bottle green, perhaps it's to do with the colour of the Vat 69 bottle, which the villains in the Hindi films of my youth used to drink. Then I remembered the men in green and my journey past the corridor to the balcony. I remembered the Reebok shoe. My mind was simultaneously hazy and clear. I saw that my friends had brought flowers and fruit, and made the room look festive and fresh, which was quite a feat considering the kind of room it was.

Needless to say, my sons had not yet arrived: two of them had sent telegrams, and the third was due to arrive in Delhi the day after. I was alive, my left breast was bandaged up and it hurt, but not unbearably. The anaesthesia didn't wear off completely for two whole days, my mouth felt dry and my stomach was distended beyond belief, and I felt bewildered by my circumstances. I sensed that Udit was in the room. His presence was gentle and quiet, his luminous eyes looked at me with puzzlement and pain, and he was telling me something that I was too hazy to grasp.

I felt better on the third day; they took the drip away, and I ate the hospital food—the jelly, the custard and the dal, in that order. I looked around for Udit, but he wasn't there, and I felt oddly let down. My friends were very quiet, they looked subdued, and I could see that Roshni, my best friend, had been crying. My son was arriving, he was taking the flight from Sweden, but nobody was going to the airport to pick him up.

When he strode into the room, my son looked so strong, so alive, so vital, that I could feel my depleted energies recharge at the very sight of him. My breast, the one that had gone, began hurting inconsolably. I found that I was smiling. I felt foolish, and young, and hopeful.

'Hi Ma! You sure got us worried for a while,' he said with concern. When he gave me a perfunctory hug, he smelt unfamiliar, of sweat and aftershaves and airplanes. I could not smell myself or Sachin in him at all. He examined the room—the green cloth screen; the wire mesh window with the dead flies; the calendar print which had been framed and hung on the yellowing walls in an excess of optimism. He looked uncomfortable and embarrassed; his eyes were restless, they would not meet mine. But then, he was jet-lagged. I was glad, immeasurably glad, to have him near me again.

Of course he was staying in my flat, he hadn't been home in four years. I worried about what he would eat and if he would manage to find the clean towels. That's what motherhood is, one worries about these things, and I told Roshni where the key to the Godrej cupboard was, and I tried to explain to my son about the water. And I was missing Udit, I was hurt that he wasn't there.

I remembered how it had been when my son was born, he had been the youngest and I was in fact deeply disappointed, I had desperately wanted a daughter. I had stared in despair at the little reptilian protuberance that indicated his manhood, but then when I held him, my breast had begun to tingle, and I knew once again the total, self-absorbed love of motherhood.

My other son called as well, but the line was bad and my throat was still hurting from all the tubes, but the sound of his voice filled me with joy and wonder. This was my eldest son, my first-born, and I remembered how he had come hurtling into the world, the incredible ease with which I had delivered him. He had been the closest to me. He would do little things for me—make me drawings, write me poems. When his father died we had coped together, he and I. But now his voice had a faraway quality and I wondered where he was, what he was wearing, how he was looking, how he had changed in the three years I had not seen him. I recalled how he had brought his school reports to be signed, a little hesitantly, even when he had done well. He was sensitive to reprimands and very conscious, even when he was a child, of the responsibility of primogeniture.

We had a puppy named Brutus that Sachin had bought for the boys. Brutus was run over by a taxi in the lane behind our house, a mere month after Sachin died. The boys had been inconsolable, they had wept and wailed until I could stand it no longer. I had yanked my eldest out of bed—his pillow had been wet with tears—and slapped him until my palms hurt. It had been so long ago, but it should have been evident to me that day so long ago that I would lose him, I would lose them all, that that was the way it would be.

When I was finally alone in the room, examining from a great distance the wilted roses in the bouquets which my friends had brought, a pert Malayali nurse came busily into the room and introduced herself. Sister Philomena had been engaged through the nurses' bureau at the insistence of my youngest son, although my friend Roshni had already discussed it with me and we had decided against private nursing. Sister Philomena checked my charts, went through my prescriptions and then settled down on the chair beside my bed with a newspaper.

'You must get ambulatory as soon as possible, dear,' she said. She had a sweet, musical voice, and the 'dear' enchanted me. Nobody had called me 'dear' for years. I dozed off, and when I awoke, Sister Philomena was no longer in the room. A hospital nurse knocked, and came in to inform me that the other bed in the twin-bedded room was shortly to be occupied. 'Very serious case,' she said sternly, 'straight from ICU. Still critical, but we have to make accommodation somehow.'

I picked up the newspaper from the table beside my bed. Being a trained journalist, I take in a page at a time, the totality of a page, and somehow manage to read everything simultaneously. The obituaries are usually on page six, I hate obituaries, and I have schooled myself to avoid them. But when I saw Udit's face—my friend Udit Narain's face—in a black-framed box, my eyes lost focus and my head went dizzy for a few minutes before everything became blurred and I slumped back on the bed in a faint. When Sister Philomena came back from her tea, or her chat with her fellow nurses, or whatever it was that she had gone to do, she found me like that.

She checked my pulse, and slapped my face about this way and that, and suddenly I was surrounded by nurses and doctors. I felt a surge of strength and something inexplicably propelled me up. I was sitting up in bed before the startled doctors, and then I was standing up. I pushed them aside, shoved them, literally, as they tried to restrain me, and walked to the corridor outside, although my legs were wobbly and I was barefoot. I walked to the end of the corridor and out past the lobby to the other side where the OT was. Sister Philomena was following me, she was holding my hand, urging me to return to the room, but I knew where it was I had to go.

When I saw the Reebok shoe lying on the ledge below the balcony, I felt a joy I cannot describe, a connectedness, a certainty, a sense of relief so immense that I actually collapsed into Sister Philomena's arms. She was a competent nurse, she got hold of a wheelchair and manoeuvred me past the milling crowds of despairing friends and relatives back to my room where, behind the bottle-green cloth screen, a very old man was being given oxygen.

When my son returned in the evening, he told me I was looking distinctly better. I smiled at him and reached out for his hand, and he looked startled and yet grateful for the gesture.

My friend Udit, Udit Narain, was run over by a redline bus on the crossing outside AIIMS. He must have been coming to visit me. I wanted above all things to see him once again, to look into those gentle, luminous eyes, and to tell him that I understood, at last, how contemplating life on Mars could put things into perspective, here, in New Delhi.

The Habit of Love

The habit of grief can be as insidious as the habit of love. When I was a young girl, I met a young man. We fell in love, we married, we had children, we fought, we stuck together, and now he was dead and I was grieving in an internal way that was eating my insides, leaving me sick, nauseous, raw and corroded. None of this showed on the outside. I looked normal and composed, like anybody one would meet anywhere, yet I inhabited an endless tunnel of grief and I was travelling it alone.

I sensed that there was something cloying, something fetid, in my mourning. In my stubborn refusal to look at sunsets, sunflowers, soap operas or seductive men—there was fear, not grief, fear that my love for him, the only bulwark of my life, might also collapse in the ceaseless flow

17

of the present. My two daughters belonged to the present, they tethered me to now with a vague, anxious sense of duty and commitment.

In the vacations, I took them for a holiday to Nepal. The three of us together shared a disconnectedness. Like three helium balloons bobbing disconsolately against a low ceiling, tangled rather than tied together by our floating strings. Two days into our four-day-three-night holiday package, we went on a mountain flight on a doubtful-looking plane: an hour's excursion between the spectacular snow peaks. 'The highest mountains in the world' as the enthusiastic in-flight brochure quite correctly called them. As for me, I didn't even want to look out, my eyes hurt from the glow and the burden of unshed tears, and the white spread of the Himalayan ranges seemed to reflect the cold expanse of pain within me. The jumbled-up lot of tourists around us—the ever-curious Gujaratis and the earnest Japanese and the honeymooning couples with dark rings under their eyes—was crowding around the window seats and clicking away with cameras. We had forgotten our own camera at the hotel and, midway through the flight, we gave up trying to match the glistening snow peaks with the names and pictures in the brochure. Always, after a while, everything begins to look the same.

The Himalayas are young mountains, they are still growing, they are exuberant, brash, unhumbled by erosion and the eventual victory of time. Eight of the world's highest mountains stood before us. The eternal snows glittered and glimmered in the sun, even as the brochures on our laps listed out their altitudes, longitudes, latitudes, their names.

'Does a mountain know its name, Mama?' my younger daughter asked. This was the sort of question my husband would have found original and I found exhausting. 'Mama, how does a mountain know it is a mountain?' she asked again, changing the inflection of the question somewhat.

'It doesn't, darling, it doesn't know its name—people give these names to them,' I said, concealing my weariness with a patient smile.

'Then I'll name them myself,' she said, in the sort of bright child's voice I found particularly tiring. The sacred peaks of Gauri Shankar, the ultimate union of Shiva and Shakti, flesh and spirit—this, my daughter decided to call the hammer and pail. Melungtse was a chocolate cake, and Ama, a crooked tooth. They had both joined in the game now. The huge massif that forms the Annapoorna range also pleased them. To them, Annapoorna I, II, and IV sounded like a WASP American family.

Of course, Everest was a disappointment, institutions always are. The name Everest was a little boring, but the Tibetan name, Chomolungma, charmed them. The Nepalese call it Sagarmatha, the buttermilk churn, in deference to Hindu mythology. There was indeed an ocean here once, and these mountains must have churned their way up, triumphantly proclaiming their mastery over the land and the waters.

'Sagarmatha is a perfect name for a mountain!' my daughter exclaimed. 'And it even looks like the wooden thingy we have in the kitchen.' My other daughter declared that she would perhaps name her daughter Sagarmatha, when and if she had a daughter. Then they were both distracted by the great beauty of Kanchenjunga which, to be honest, is the most appropriate name possible for that golden peak. Makulu had something playful about it, 'like a monkey,' and we landed in Kathmandu quite unable to fault the locals in their faculty for naming mountain peaks.

That night, alone in my bed in the untidy hotel room, surrounded by scattered clothes and strewn socks, I stayed awake late into the night, listening with an unnamed fear to the steady breaths of their healthy young bodies. When at last I fell asleep, I dreamt of an unnamed mountain, surrounded by fog and clouds and mist, a lonely mountain, a mountain without a name. I awoke with a start to the safe sounds of my daughters' steady breathing. I was both sad and exhilarated and for some reason I was reminded of the time of the power cuts when we all used to sleep on our terrace in Delhi, the four of us, my husband, my daughters and me. Our house was on the outskirts of town, near the airport, and at night the sky would be vivid with stars, broken by the broad beams of the aeroplane lights as they readied for landing.

When the electricity failed—which was often—we would troop out on to the terrace, skin damp with mosquito repellent, and try to fall asleep to the soft humming of the mosquito clouds that hovered above us. We would gaze at the constellations spread across the darkening sky above us, the heady fragrance of chameli and frangipani and raat ki raani leavening the night. Only my husband knew the names of the constellations—Orion, the Great Bear, the Pleiades. I knew their Indian names. For Hindus, the Great Bear is the Saptarishi, the seven sacred sages from whom the brahmins were descended, and then there was the Pole Star, the Dhruv Tara, a constant in a changing world.

My daughters, with their untutored minds, saw things differently. For them, Orion was a crooked bed frame, a skewered celestial version of the squat wooden charpoy on which we sleep out in the open. The Pleiades were 'the pincushion' and as for the Great Bear, Ursa Major—my younger daughter insisted on calling it 'the Question Mark'. I thought then, in the way mothers do, that she was brilliant, and destined for great things for, clearly, Ursa Major looked more like a question mark than a bear, great or small.

Of course, the constellations looked different when they were named: time and space and motion and the distortions of perception—all these things ensure the mismatch between names and things. The past inhabits the future just as the future looms over the past. Names are not just labels or conveniences, they carry with them the magical conviction of the power of naming, allied to the power of knowing. Mountains, constellations, emotions—they have an existence all their own, we only seek to appropriate them with words.

It was dawn, the first flush of morning light could be seen through the window of the hotel room. I fell asleep again, and once again I dreamt of that mountain, which kept vigil over a bank of clouds, a lonely mountain, a mountain without a name. Perhaps I went on to dream of other things, I don't really remember, but when I awoke it was with a sense of clarity and purpose. The sun was streaming in through the window, and my daughters were still asleep, their blankets tossed away, their strong young limbs tangled. In the clear light of day, I knew what I had not known the night before. I knew the name of the mountain of which I had dreamt. Naming things makes them tidy, manageable, complete.

The name of the mountain was grief.

Chronicles of Exile

I have only just heard the news. My Queen Qandhari is dead. She walked into a forest fire with her husband, King Dhritarashtra and her sister-in-law Kunti. The court is in mourning. The priests are orating the funerary prayers. The common people, or what is left of them, are shaken, bewildered. This self-immolation marks the end of an age, a yuganta.

This city has seen enough death. After the war, for months, bodies lay strewn on the battlefield at Kurukshetra. Hyenas would dart out from the forest and make off with an arm, a leg, or a mass of flesh that could have been anything at all. There was no wood in Hastinapura to burn the dead. Two or three logs are not enough to cremate the body of a warrior. Widows would sort through the mess of dismembered corpses to search for their husbands, and often their sons as well. They would hold up a decomposed hand to see from the rings or the scars on the wrist if they knew it. They would examine those dead bodies with wonder, as if they could not remember or believe that they had once been ordinary women, who had held those men in their arms, and been held by them, and borne them children.

They would try to burn the bodies with straw, but it would smoke and the fire would not catch. The old men went to the forest as far off as the Dwaitavana but the wood they brought back was young, the sap still rising in it. The smell of rot and death was in our nostrils, and the damp smoke from the funeral fires had settled like a miasma over the untended pleasure gardens, the abandoned sabha ghars, the lonely palaces. In the humble houses of the poor, the smell of rice cooking would gladden the hearth, and sometimes the laughter of a child would break the sorrowing silence, but in the palaces, the children were all dead, and the young men as well. Now, the old people, Dhritarashtra, his Queen Qandhari, and the queen mother Kunti have died, consumed by a forest fire.

She must have sensed the fire before the others did for, although her eyes were bandaged, her faculties were sharper than those of most others. She would have heard and understood the first warning—the cries of birds as they circled the high trees. Walking into the flames could only have been her idea. Qandhari always had a streak of perversity in her; it was in her nature to swim against the current, to be contrary, make things difficult for herself.

Kunti was different, a survivor; after those years when her sons were in exile, she knew better than to court danger. I never knew two women so different. But they were both strong, and stubborn.

Kunti walked into the fire with my mistress Qandhari, as did blind Dhritarashtra. Servants know their masters better than they know themselves, anticipating their mistakes as keenly as their wishes. Qandhari never punished me except once. That was her gracious privilege, but life had punished her fiercely. A hundred sons, and only one living—no one deserves so much pain. I have not slept since I heard the news.

I have not eaten or slept since I heard the news. My fingers, once so nimble, have not held a comb for five years now. My queen, whom I served all my life, whose tresses I combed and oiled and braided, and saw turn grey and then white, is dead. Only I knew how to singe the split hairs in her braid with the quick sure strokes of a glowing incense stick. Now, with her sister-in-law Kunti, she has abandoned the call of the living, and stepped of her own will into a blazing river of fire. As the snakes slithered away from their burrows, and the monkeys and langurs clambered across the fevered limbs of incandescent trees, and the birds circled and grieved for their young who could not fly, and watched their nests turn molten, Qandhari stepped into the flames to learn the knowledge of light.

Kunti followed her. When she was young, this same Kunti had rejected the flames, stepped away from the pyre where her husband Pandu lay burning. She had embraced life even as her co-wife Madri decided to die with Pandu. She walked away from the funeral flames, comforting her weeping sons, Yudhisthira, Bhima, Arjuna, Nakula and Sahadeva. Nakula and Sahadeva were born of Madri's womb, but Kunti loved them all the more for that. Now those boys have destroyed the pride of our race, they have killed my queen's hundred sons, and they rule victorious over Hastinapura. Yet their mother Kunti chose to walk into the fire with my queen. I ask you, why?

As for that old man Dhritarashtra, I cannot bear to think about him. We should never have left Qandahara. We should not have allowed ourselves to be lured by his gold and caskets of jewels to leave the mountains. What did we lack there? Nothing! We lacked nothing. The snow mountains gave us their blessing, and we had an abundance of fruits and flowers through the seasons. The air kissed and caressed our skins like a lover. There was always a fragrance of roses in the air, and the sweet sting of pine. In summer, the mountains shimmered in the haze, and by the evening, a cool breeze would revive the city. My princess would throw open the window of her turret room. She would instruct me to unbraid her hair, and we would sit together by the window, and I would untangle and comb her locks even as the wind tangled them together again.

I was younger than her, but I remember everything about Qandahara, although the memories have lost their clarity from being remembered too much. It was not hot and dusty as it is here in Hastinapura, and we were deceived in our decision to come here. Bhishma's lying messengers came to us carrying gifts and gold. There was a nightingale in a gilded cage and a mynah that could talk like a man, or bark like a dog. Qandhari was amused by these gifts, but it was her father who decided, and the gold decided him.

King Suballa came into her room that afternoon, as she sat by the window, staring out at the snow mountains, as I untangled her hair. I rose nervously to my feet, for the king had never visited his daughter in her chamber before. 'You are to be married to Dhritarashtra, the king of Hastinapura,' he announced, in a voice far sterner than the occasion demanded.

'And is he handsome?' my princess asked. Her eyes were alight with excitement, and her enchanting dimpled smile broke across her face like a sunrise.

'So I am told,' said her father. 'You shall leave tomorrow. Your brother Zakuni shall accompany you, and any two of your maids you wish to take with you.'

'I shall take Zara,' my princess announced excitedly. 'Will you come with me, Zara? Say that you will, please!'

'I shall do as my princess desires,' I replied formally, for I was in the presence of the king, and quaking with fear lest I do or say something wrong.

'It's hot in the summer there,' the king remarked, 'although the winters are cool. See that you pack some splendid clothes for my daughter.'

I was overwhelmed. The king had never spoken to me before. 'Certainly I shall, Your Majesty,' I murmured, bowing as low as I possibly could. Suballa turned around regally and left the room. Qandhari was laughing and weeping at the same time. We called for her maid and began going through trunks and wardrobes. To burnish her locks, for an aureole around her head, I packed eleven vials of golden lac powder. Forbidden to all but royalty, this lac is extracted from rare mountain scarabs. Roasted on slow fires for a month and a week, this precious concoction can make even the dullest hair gleam and shine with a halo, competing with golden crowns and jewelled coronets.

That evening, Qandhari went to her royal mother's chambers to bid her goodbye. The queen had been ailing for a long time, from a mysterious disease no royal physician could diagnose. Her nose would bleed incessantly for days on end. Strange welts and bruises would appear all over her pale body of their own accord. She would feel faint when she lay down and dizzy if she got up. She had an unending litany of contrary symptoms which she guarded with stubborn patience, even as sorcerers, shamans, witches and astrologers from across the land tried to demonstrate their prowess and win the favour of the king.

We tiptoed in together. The air in the darkened room was still and heavy with the smell of stale incense and potions and distilled medicinal oils. The queen examined her daughter mournfully. Her face was enormous and bloated, her eyes sunk in a well of dark shadows. 'So, you are to be married,' she said tentatively. 'It is not easy to be a queen. Perhaps your beauty will captivate him.' Then she closed her eyes again, and pretended to be asleep. We rushed out and gulped the fresh air in the corridor.

The young people held a celebration that evening to bid Qandhari goodbye. It was only the princesses and their cousins. One of the boys played the flute while the girls sang songs of love. He was slim and beautiful, his eyes lined with long, dark lashes. We sipped sweet mead and by the end of it, everyone was slightly drunk. The flute player was casting bold eyes at my mistress. She was returning his advances with coy glances, and I hurried her back to her room; we didn't want any trouble the night before we were to leave.

I lost count of the days we travelled. First the high mountains, on horseback, for Qandhari had learnt to ride almost before she could walk, and then in litters through the high passes. The men negotiated the impossibly rocky terrain, holding the horses by the reins and leading them on foot. I kept away from Zakuni. He had a reputation for being nasty, and the king was well rid of him in the palace, though what we would do with him in Hastinapura I did not know.

In the kingdom of Salya, the king of Hastinapura had sent two elephants and a chariot to receive our party. Now, Zakuni was a pale, slender young man and when he saw the enormous animals he went pale with fear. He sat in the chariot with the women, and I was careful to keep my distance from him. It was whispered in Qandahara that he had tried to poison his elder brother so that he might be anointed crown prince. No one dared to say it aloud, but we knew it nevertheless. He had a way of looking up suddenly and catching your eye that was quite unnerving.

My princess had lost weight during the journey, she had become thin and her hair was lank and limp. She rarely smiled, and there were dark shadows settling down on her young face, a premonition of her mother's haunted expression.

When we finally arrived in Hastinapura, we were welcomed at the north gate by a musical recital of pipes and drums. They showered rose petals on our chariot. Qandhari looked tired, listless, uninterested in our new surroundings.

'We will meet your handsome husband soon,' I told her. 'You must appear shy and demure before him.'

The old queen mother, Satyavati, summoned us. She was a shrewd-looking woman with a discontented expression. Her two daughters-in-law, Ambika and Ambalika, hovered nervously by her side. Their attendants led us to our new quarters. The palace in which we were lodged was very impressive. It was built of marble and red sandstone, and had jewelled walls and deep sunken baths to luxuriate in. The water had been heated with a firestone in anticipation of our arrival, and lotus flowers floated artlessly as though in a forest pool. I was enchanted, and washed and scrubbed my princess until she could take it no more. The bed was draped with silks and peacock plumes, but she was too tired to notice, and fell asleep the moment her head touched the pillow. She slept for two nights and a day, and when she awoke, she was the old Qandhari again, bubbling with joy and infectious laughter. Her dimples came to life again, and she was impatient to be dressed and to take stock of her new surroundings.

There were several maidens who had been appointed to serve us. They dressed their hair in elaborate pretentious styles quite different from the simple flowered braids my princess favoured. They flaunted ribbons and glittering threads in their stringy hair. I knew my golden lac powder would win the show, but I could not afford to be complacent. Anxious that my princess not be considered lacking in elegance, I rushed to the marketplace to search for collyrium and silk ribbons and civet perfume. I could of course have asked the Hastinapura handmaidens to assist me, but I was eager to get a feel of our new home city.

The streets of Hastinapura were splendid, broad and gracious and neatly cobbled. I purchased all the items I needed, then stopped to haggle with a vendor of silks over some ribbons. They spoke differently here; I had difficulty understanding the language. Yet I could get by once I understood that they stressed their consonants differently. 'These ribbons are fit for a queen,' the salesman declared.

'And it is a queen who will wear them,' I countered. 'When your king sets his eyes on her, he will partake in a feast of beauty.'

The salesman's mouth fell loose from shock. 'Do you serve the new queen who has come from the north?' he asked.

'Indeed I do,' I announced proudly.

'And do you not know?' he continued nervously.

'What is it I do not know?' I inquired irritably. 'There are surely many things that could fit into this category.'

'Do you not know that our good king is blind from birth?' he asked with concern.

At first I did not understand his words, for I was unjumbling the consonants in order that I might understand them. 'Blind,' I asked stupidly. 'You mean he cannot see?'

'You do not have to pay for the ribbons,' he replied hastily. 'I have to shut my shop now.'

I held him fiercely by the wrist and accosted him. 'Is your king blind?' I said. 'Reply yes or no!'

'Yes,' he said ashamedly, as though it were somehow his fault. I thought of my princess, of her smooth skin, her carefree eyes, her dimpled smile, and a deep sorrow came and burdened itself upon my heart. 'I will protect her,' I vowed. 'I will see her through this time and we shall return together to Qandahara.' I made my way back to the palace in a daze. On the way, I met a beggar who sat on the steps, whining for alms.

'Does your king have eyes?' I asked him.

'Yes,' he replied, and an absurd ray of hope rose in my heart, 'but not such as he can see with.' He continued to opportune me for alms, but I waved him away. 'Not for such unpropitious words,' I screamed, a ball of anger rising to my throat. Who had done this to us? Did the king her father know? Did Zakuni? What had the messenger from Hastinapura told them? How much gold had he given?

My princess was examining her face in the mirror. 'Do you think he will find me beautiful?' she asked anxiously. 'I have grown too thin in this journey.'

'There is no mirror in his eyes,' I said solemnly. My words sounded strange in my ears, for it is not my habit to speak in such a stilted fashion.

Of course, she did not understand. 'There is a spot on my cheek,' she continued, 'and my skin seems to have lost its colour.'

Zakuni was standing at the doorway. He had heard me speak. An amused smile was playing on his face, as though he were anticipating an enjoyable encounter. 'Do you not understand, sister?' He said gently, too gently. 'Your husband-to-be is blind.'

She fell to the floor in a dead faint. Zakuni continued to smile. 'We are all of us blind,' he said, as though in consolation. The physicians were called in, and all her new family came to attend on her. She could neither move nor speak, although she would flutter her eyelids, and sip water if it were placed on her tongue.

They all came—Bhishma, Vidura, Satyavati, and her widowed daughters-in-law—concern and dismay on their faces. I combed her hair as she lay in bed, and she touched my arm gently in appreciation. Just then, the king walked in, the blind King Dhritarashtra to whom she was to be married. He was a handsome man in those days, tall and well-built, and he walked with the assurance of a king. Yet he stumbled and hit his leg against her bed, and the courtier who was escorting him had to guide her betrothed to her side.

'We are well pleased to have you in Hastinapura,' he said, using the royal form of address for himself. 'Evidently the journey has tired you out.'

Qandhari kept her eyes tightly shut. Her face had become a mask. She gave no reply, and the visitors tiptoed out. When they had gone, she opened her eyes and looked at me earnestly. 'There is no way out,' she said. 'If he cannot see my face, I, too, shall foreswear to see him.'

'Princess, you cannot live your life with your eyes shut!' I exclaimed.

She attempted a defiant look, although her eyes retained an expression of infinite sadness. 'I shall cover up my eyes with bandages,' she said. 'You must help me, Zara.'

I was speechless. But she was serious and full of childish purpose. 'You must get me bandages,' she urged. 'I shall give up the gift of sight. That is the only way I could live with him.'

Sometimes, we servants humour our masters, indulging the whim or tantrum of the moment, knowing well that it will pass. 'If you so desire, my princess,' I said, and began combing her hair to soothe her.

'You think this is a whim, Zara,' she said gently, 'but no, it is a vow.' I never saw her smile again.

There are some hurts that cannot be healed by courage alone. They need anger, and tears, and the consolation of love. But what could I say to her? I was a servant. I went, as instructed, to buy her bandages.

*

Swathed around her eyes was the softest, lightest, whitest silk I could find. I circled her thrice and closed her eyes forever. We would change the bandages every full moon, at night. Outside. She would keep her eyes shut. Was she never tempted to open them?

They got along well as a couple; they had children, so, evidently, that worked between them. A hundred and one children, a daughter and a hundred sons. Of course, she loved Duryodhana the most, and he knew it. 'My firstborn,' she would murmur, and my eyes fill up with tears here and now as I remember her voice when she said that. She longed to see him, she would stroke his face over and over again when he was a baby. To memorize it. Duryodhana, Dussala, Dussana. These were her favourites among her children.

The daughter Dussala, I used to comb her hair every night. I would stroke and smooth and pull, oil it weekly, wash it with a gentle lather of reetha pods, but it remained listless. It had no life in it, no body. She was a plain-looking princess, that's all there was to it. Unlike Draupadi, the princess married to Kunti's five sons. I used to comb her hair, too, sometimes, in the old days. It was as though someone had oiled a streak of lightning and contained it in a cloud. She was proud of her hair, she would play with it for effect, even though she knew it drove the men around her mad. She was like that. I'm not sure whether I liked her but I admired her. I did. I taught her how to double-braid her hair, and knot it into elaborate rolls, and other tricks of the trade.

When the Pandavas were in exile, when—let's face it— Duryodhana and his brothers had tricked and cheated their cousins, when Kunti's sons wandered through the land like beggars even though they were born of kings and royal blood, Draupadi worked as a hairdresser in the Virata court, for queen Sudeshna. The men didn't leave her alone there, either, Sudeshna's brother Keechaka made advances at her, and Bhima killed him. Bhima would.

She did something to men. There was something defiant about her beauty, and it drove them mad. Dussala's husband, Jayadratha, was another one. Couldn't she see what she was doing to them? Was she blind?

That day, in court, when her husband Yudhisthira gambled her away, and Dussana pulled her by her long dark hair, her hair that had been purified by sacred waters during the Rajasuya yagya, and tried to undrape her clothes, Vidura shut his eyes in horror. He chose not to see what had happened.

Draupadi had been for her ritual bath after her menses that day. Her hair was damp, that's why it was left loose, not set into the elaborate coiffed plait that she normally favoured. She thought the style gave her height, but she was wrong, it made her appear too tall, too commanding for a woman, even for a royal.

My Queen Qandhari had decided to become blind a long time ago. That day, her blindness infected all her family, a swift epidemic. I did not ever discuss the incident with her, it was not my place to do so, but we whispered about it in the kitchens and washrooms. We were all shamed by it—a blind king and a queen who chose to be blind, and their sons whose strength strengthened before the weak.

I am told that she tried to take off the bandages once, when they had retreated to the mountains together. Dhritarashtra and Qandhari and Kunti. The old king and his queen had lost a hundred sons, and Kunti, the queen mother now, had lost Kaunteya, the most beloved of her children. Better to be a poor beggar with lice in your hair than live in palaces and know such grief. But they recovered in the mountains. It was a novelty not to have servants, though they were, of course, invisibly in place—Kunti's royal sons and daughter-in-law had ensured that. The old people ate fruits from the trees and sighed with the mountain breezes, and their sorrows seemed distant for a while. She took them off when they went on a picnic and the sharp scent of pine needles reminded my Queen Qandhari of our home in the mountains, before she was brought here as Dhritarashtra's wife.

'I wish I could see the pine trees,' she'd said wistfully, in her gentle voice with that edge of reproach in it. Dhritarashtra lost his temper, he start raging at her. 'Have I ever stopped you? Did I instruct you to tie your eyes up? Was it my whim? '

'I did it for you!' she had exclaimed.

'The noble queen Qandhari!' he had retorted.

Kunti tried to calm them down, but they were fighting like a pair of children. Qandhari was throwing one of her famous sulks, and Dhritarashtra had completely lost control.

'Did the king your father tell my father, the royal Suballa, that you were blind?'

'You have blinded me twice over, my queen! Did you ever think to ask me how I felt, when you tied your eyes up with a silly rag of silk? You should have been my saviour! I could have looked at life through your eyes. But no! You had to make a virtue of your cowardice.'

Kunti, always practical, always well meaning, had undone her bandages. The sunlight dazzled my queen's orbs, but she, who had lost the habit of vision, saw nothing but blinding light around her.

'I, too, have been blinded twice, my lord,' Qandhari had said to her husband, gravely and courteously. They did not fight after that, I am told, but retreated into their customary courtesy. It was not as though they did not love each other; they were a mirror of their faults and fears.

*

Qandahara. Qum. Qabul. All so far away now. Yet I remain loyal to my Queen Qandhari. There are eleven vials of golden lac powder I have guarded through my life, but have no one to anoint them with.

'Time leaves nothing true,' the priests declared, at the funeral orations for the two queens. And for Dhritarashtra, but I do not care to remember him.

As the fire crackled, and the twigs hissed and remembered the time of green leaves, I knew the priests were wrong. Death is always true, as is war. And love?

Grand Hotel I

The Children

Grand Hotel, Nainital. In the year 1964, it is a 'modern' hotel, with concrete and cement staircases and balustrades, not wood. It is just off the lake, above the Mall Road. A long veranda runs along the length of the hotel, on the ground floor and the first floor.

There is a wooden table and two chairs outside each room. Vinita is seated outside room 136—it is a suite—overlooking the lake. The lights from the Ayarpatta side are reflecting in the waves, streaks of silver in the blue-black water. It is May in Nainital, the height of the summer season. 27 May 1964. Jawaharlal Nehru had died of a heart

45

attack that morning, and the hill station town of Nainital is in mourning.

That is what Vinita is thinking, as she sits on the chair by the veranda and looks at the lake. 'Chacha Nehru died this morning, and now the nation is in mourning.' She has a way with words, even then, and is destined to become a writer. In her mind, in her thoughts, 'morning' and 'mourning' are in italics, in a cursive script.

Vinita sighs, looks at the lake, and at the moon. It is a full moon, sitting ochre and low above the opposite hill. Its jaundiced face is not reflected in the lake. 'Chacha Nehru was a great leader of our Nation. He loved Children and believed that they are the Future of India.' That is how Vinita's essay on Pandit Jawaharlal Nehru, to be penned on 14 November, will begin. Children's Day is still far in the future, on this day when Vinita is vacillating between 'Children' and 'the Children'. *He loved the Children and believed they are the Future of India.* On reflection, she scratches out 'the' with a neat stroke of her fountain pen, on that day when she writes the essay on Chacha Nehru.

On the 27th of May, with the almost-full moon hovering over the lake, Vinita weeps as she thinks of Chacha Nehruji and his love for children. Everybody in Nainital is weeping, huddling over crackling radios, listening to the news on the BBC. Or Akashvani. They speak to each other in hushed whispers. In the Grand Hotel, the sense of shared loss has led to a sort of funereal camaraderie, with social barriers dissolving, if not disappearing. The head cook is so distraught that he has not yet begun to make dinner. Hungry guests are being served leftovers from the larder or the Westinghouse refrigerator. They are sobbing and sniffling over watered tomato soup as they remember Pandit Nehru and his greatness.

'He was so handsome,' Vinita's mother, Renuka Mehta, whispers brokenly. 'The handsomest man I ever saw. Who can ever replace Nehru? Not Shastri . . . he's a dwarf, a midget, not even five feet tall!' And she breaks down, dabbing her eyes with the pallav of her elegant cotton sari, ruining it with smears of black eyeliner.

They are listening to the BBC, not All India Radio. Vinita's father, Mr Mehta, is thumbing his Japanese transistor radio in frustration. It is in a leatherette case with holes in it, so that you can listen right through it. But it isn't working, so they are listening to the bulky Murphy in the bedroom of their hotel suite, while their daughter Vinita sits in the veranda looking at the lake and the moon.

Mrs and Mr Mehta are building up to a quarrel, to the periodical bloodletting that allows them to continue within the constraints of their arranged marriage. Vinita's father resented the remark about Shastri being a dwarf, a midget. He is a short man himself, shorter than his wife. His mother has requested her daughter-in-law not to wear high heels as women shouldn't ever look taller than their husbands. Vinita's mother Renuka has resolutely ignored this outrageous suggestion. She is a tough woman even though she is weeping tonight for Pandit Nehru.

The transistor batteries have clearly packed up, and this has only added to Mr Mehta's sense of things falling apart. He pours himself a whisky, and even as he is doing so, there is a power breakdown. The radio crackles to a halt. In Parliament, announcing the news of the prime minister's death, C. Subramanium has said. 'The light has gone out.' Mr Mehta remembers that as the soda water he is pouring into the whisky splashes onto his shoes in the dark.

The fight between them builds up, in the dark, in the silence. It is bitter and pointless and has an edge of hopelessness to it. Vinita's mother decides to have a rum and coke. They argue in low whispers and Renuka Mehta continues to weep for Pandit Nehru, whom she had met once many years ago at an Army Raising Day when her father had been the commanding officer. The light has gone out.

Outside, on the veranda, Vinita is still watching the moon. It has moved higher in the sky, and the Nainital lake is holding its reflection in a mirror embrace. It is getting cold on the veranda, but it is too dark to go in and hunt for a cardigan. Vinita has a thing for numbers, and she is calculating in her head how many years Chacha Nehru spent in this world. Seventy-four years, six months and thirteen days, she concludes. Then she tries to calculate how long she has spent in this world, loses interest, and starts to think about death. Death is a dark blob over Nainital, and over India, today.

Her shoes are hurting but they are too pretty to be abandoned. Blue ballet shoes. She has not told her mother that they are too tight for her. She can hear her parents arguing in the sitting room of the hotel suite. She knows that tone of voice and has learnt to keep away when she hears it. She stops thinking about death and looks again at the moon. For the first time in her life, ever, she can see the rabbit on it, the alert ears, the crouched body. Vinita smiles at the moon as a waiter places a candle on the table on the veranda. He lights it and asks her if she wants anything. She says no. He pats her on her shoulder and leaves. They are sharing in the sorrow of India.

The lights have come back on the other end of Nainital, in Tallital, and half the lake is once again streaked with zigzag reflections on rippling water.

It is as though there were a tide inside Vinita sweeping her out of the veranda, down the steps, to a patch of lawn beneath a deodar tree. She takes the candle with her, and a blanket from her bedroom next to the suite where her parents are still arguing in whispers. She lays the blanket on the soft summer grass and carefully places the candle on a flat boulder. At the stroke of the midnight hour, when the world sleeps, she can hear dogs howling, as though in a chorus, and then one by one, hill to hill, in fierce competition. There is a whir of wings in the distant branches of the deodar tree above her. A monkey, a bat, a ghost. She looks at the candle and smiles. The smile is for Chacha Nehru, who loves the children and believes that they are the future of India.

Grand Hotel II

The Other Shore

At Lake Como, towards the shores of Lago di Lecco, the granddaughter walks along the waterfront. The Metropole, the Grand, the Suisse, the Splendide. Hotel du Lac. They are all shuttered, closed, readying for the season. *Arriveste Prima Vera,* the signs read. Opening in Spring. The Hotel du Lac is enclosed in scaffolding. The Splendide is being painted, this year's blue a shade darker and deeper than that of the previous season. The Suisse has one guest, a straggler who has stayed on. The guest watches the granddaughter stare at the deserted lakeshore. He wonders where she is from, what she is doing here. Her sari flutters in the fierce breeze, like a rising, circling gull. In her mind's eye she is on the Mall Road, at home in Nainital, clutching her grandmother's hand as they walk from the Grand Hotel towards the Metropole.

'All tourist towns are schizophrenic,' her uncle had observed, on that long-ago day when she had first learnt to swim. 'Especially colonial hill stations.' Here, today, by the shores of Lake Como, she remembers her grandmother's gaze, wary, disapproving, as she had floundered in the waters. Too young to wear a brassiere, she had stripped down to her nylon knickers and tiptoed into the water, encouraged by her cousins.

Her grandmother, whom she called mother, *Ija*, was born by the shores of Naukuchiyatal lake. 'The lake is full of snakes,' her Ija had told her, 'harmless water snakes, but I was afraid, and the servants would carry me from the house to the lake shore, on their shoulders, and place me safely in the boat. I would row across alone after that.' Her grandmother's grey-green eyes, like the lake shore, then and here.

'Bellisimo,' an old lady murmurs. The whisper of the waters rises to a roar. There is a storm gathering.

The eyes of old women, worn, wet, nested. Her grandmother lies dying, in a mountain town on another continent, by a lakeside rubbled with tourists' relics. In the shabby hospital fronted by the splendidly large statue of her grand uncle, the freedom fighter, her grandmother can no longer hear the waves. The rain is cascading on the tin roof, like artillery fire, but she cannot hear that, either.

The grandmother's eyes, cradled in shadows, are open, but she does not see her daughter, who is staring at her with concern, and the faint, unexpressed hope that it will soon be over, painlessly. She sees the noble leader of the people, not his stone statue grotesquely crafted, but the man himself, her brother the great politician, with his storm of white hair and his scornful mouth hidden under a greying moustache. Her eyelids flicker, and the movement alerts her daughter, alarms her. The daughter rushes off to call a nurse, a doctor, someone who can seal this unfinished transaction with the past.

In the grandmother's memories, in the granddaughter's dreams, they are in Nainital, walking up from the Grand Hotel to the Metropole. The great man is addressing a political meeting in the football grounds. The stadium is full, as it usually is in the summer months: for political rallies, for inter-state hockey tournaments, for fiercely fought football honours. The great man is addressing the expectant crowds, his fine mane of snowy hair flying this way and that as his scornful eyes become momentarily dreamy. 'And this is what I have to say to you.' He addresses the sea of faces, searching out the very pupils of their eyes; they are turning rapturous in response to the dreams billowing from his voice, bellowing from the megaphone with a hint of reverb, echoed by the hill-peaks around—China Peak, Tiffin Top, Snow View. 'That this land of ours, this sacred soil of Kumaon, is the dev bhoomi, the land of the gods themselves!'

Then wind rises on the lake. A flash of lightning and sheets of rain marching in graded formation down from the heights of China Peak towards the football field by the lake. The leader of the people confronts the rain with disdain, his eyes sweeping over the crowds, and he continues speaking, softly, slowly, seductively. It is a challenge to keep the crowds there, with him, listening to his dreams.

The grandmother, who had led the girl there to hear him speak, is alarmed by the rain. She reaches for the folded umbrella in her bag. The granddaughter's summer frock, a powdery pink, matches her flowered chiffon sari. Taking the girl firmly by the hand, she leads her towards the Metropole, where they are to have lunch. She has escaped her grand uncle, but he still has the crowds in thrall. The rain is pouring down on them, on his dreams, but they are spellbound, they do not stir. The people have risen to the bait of their greatness, of his scornful eyes.

As they walk towards the Metropole the rain falls harder, harsher, and before the girl's amazed eyes it has turned white. Pebbles the colour of clouds pelt the Flats and the football grounds. The lakeside promenade is covered with sleet and frozen rain. The tourists are gaping with

enthusiasm, wide-mouthed. This is a bonus. The political meeting is breaking up. Reluctantly, the great man leaves the podium. 'Is this snow?' the girl asks her grandmother. She tilts the umbrella towards her granddaughter and begins to walk even faster.

*

'Is this snow, Ija?' I ask. She shakes her head, abstracted.

After a brief pause she says, 'No, it's not snow, you silly. It's hail.'

After lunch, we walk towards the temple of Naina Devi. The hailstorm has subsided. Outside the arched doorway are the lepers, beggars and vagrants. A woman with sunken eyes and hair like a crown of matted straw is holding a naked child to her breast. My grandmother looks at her, and then at me. She shakes off her soft pashmina shawl and drapes it around the baby. She clicks her hand bag open and takes out some money. Notes, not change. These she drops into the worn tin container placed before the beggar woman. Then, her eyes hardening, she clutches me by the shoulder and herds me into the temple.

The other beggars, their alms tins full of hailstones, set up a clamour, beseeching her pity, but the border of her pink chiffon sari is already drenched and she rushes me into the temple. My grandmother does not believe in God at large, or in the individual goddess whose shelter we are seeking.

She is unmoved by the gold-plated statue of Nanda Devi, ignores her fierce painted eyes, the third eye leaping like a fish between her brows. She leads me to shelter, ignoring the phallus of Shiva, turning her back to Rama and Sita, so that we can view the hailstones pock the rippled lake. I have been to the temple before, many times, with my ayah Saruli. She has told me of the other temple, in the depths of the lake, deep below, where two giant fish guard the actual, living goddess.

The blustering wind moves and shakes the temple bells, as here, in Lake Como, the church bells mark the Angelus. We are both there together, my grandmother and I, by the lake's shore, until the church bells shake me from my reverie.

The boulders of pain in my heart are ground to a keen, fine intensity. Under the flying wind, feathered by squawking ducks, is a heap of empty snail shells. A wasp buzzes contentedly inside one of them. I examine the coiled symmetry of the fragile shells, and ponder the nature of mollusc defences. We all have to some day leave our armour behind.

I wander up the hillside, around the gardens of Bellagio about to break into blossom—crocus, narcissus, iris, tubers renewed in the warming soil of springtime. There, in the familiar landscape of lake and mountain slope, the fussily tended garden path curves around the slanting mountain to slink into disrepair. 'Do not enter', a sign declares, provocatively, seductively.

I recognize these caveats, having painted them with as much determination across labyrinthine memory lanes. Sometimes, one may ignore these warnings, take the untended path across the uncertain road, but I turned my attention firmly to the present. Settling myself on a stone bench, placed to capture the vista of sky and slope and wave, I extract a book from my handbag, yet another forbidding text on postcolonialism. As I prepare to enter into its dense verbiage, the handwritten lines in the margin of the opening chapter draw my attention. 'The world, including the emotional world of lovers, and the psychic universe of the world, is inherently entropic.' Then the words wander off to the other edge of the page, under the title, pencilled in a whispering, slanted handwriting, insidiously overwriting the black Garamond typeface of the purposeful text: Things fall apart, people die, memories fade.

*

The grandmother floats in and out of lives, dreams chasing nightmares in monotonous succession. It is as if Ija were on stage, perhaps the Ramlila stage in Mallital where, during Dussehra, she would watch the annual battle between good and evil enacted in the market square from the bedroom window of her friend the Sahji's wife. Ancient memory has unexpected trapdoors, and stage exits disguised as forests or palace entrances. Suddenly she is by the lake shore, observing a dragonfly dry its wings, and then my mother's voice, harsh and commanding, inquiring about her health.

'I am well,' she replies formally, and a little stiffly, to indicate her dislike for her bossy elder daughter. The child was never her favourite, but all the rest are dead, and she is bonded in helplessness to her stern keeper.

Ija hears a hoot of laughter, and the demons are returning to the stage, executing a circuitous dance, graceful and compelling. Grateful and compelling? She cannot remember, there are no connects in her memory, only a sliding play of remembered thoughts, repeating themselves in random symmetry.

She could think long thoughts once, complete thoughts, but now they condense like clouds around her—joy, sometimes, or anger, often despair. The night-time hurts more, every memory of pain and injury coming alive, never happiness. She is trapped in her body, in this moment, in the changing weather.

The dragonfly has dried its wings, the demons have stopped dancing, stopped calling, only her daughter opens the door to check if she is all right, if she is still alive.

*

Hence, in my world, in a room by the lake my lover marks me with his anger and his need. It is urgent and greedy and relentless, his need to reach out to me. But I am tangled in the past, in memories and time loops, trapped in the many dimensions of nowhere. I watch him as though from a great distance. It is only the next day, in the afternoon, awaking from the tired sleep of evasion, that my body responds to his remembered caress.

His nails have drawn blood from my cunt, the blood and wetness and shyness all a mess of moisture and stain on the sheets. His anger and his need. His hurts.

Paralysed, I cannot run away from or towards him. I love him, he loves me, but there are things neither he nor I can leave behind.

My grandmother is still lost in time, immobilized in another lifetime. Her eyes glazed with the knowledge of death. 'Won't you please eat something?' she asks me tenderly. Her gown has lifted above her thighs. She is almost naked. I can recognize my legs, my crotch, my dented breasts; I have inherited them from her.

Left behind, he feels left behind. His sperm swims up my thighs, to reclaim what was once his, suddenly nobody's. He leaves his sperm behind. We have hurt each other, and known the reassurance of pain.

My grandmother's body is like mine. I feel the shock of recognition, a glimpse of the future, of collapse and death. Her toothless gums bared in tenderness. Suddenly I am hungry for my lover, I need his touch, I want to hurt, be hurt, to remember only my body. Rejection is sometimes a form of recognition. When we first made love, on a perfect day, by a stream in the mountains, mysteriously in spate despite the summer drought, he matched his burnt brown skin with my pale one. 'You are almost the same colour as I!' he exclaimed in wonderment.

I turned to him in surprise, reading colour in his words, racism, the burden of colonial rule.

I walk past the Grand Hotel, the Swiss, the Splendide, Hotel du Lac. A harsh wind rises from the shores of Lake Como. In India, in the Himalayas, in Nainital, my grandmother dreams on. She lies on the hospital bed, hoisted to an improbable angle by a thoughtful nursing assistant. She is walking from the Grand Hotel towards the Metropole. They stop at the temple, she and her granddaughter. She sees a beggar woman approaching, with sunken eyes and hair like a crown of matted straw, a naked baby in her arms. She reaches out for the money in her bag. But no, it is not that. The child is smiling, and the woman's hands, as she leads my grandmother away, are firm, kindly and decisive.

Omens I

Vatsala Vidyarthi was a literary lady. She had eyes like almonds, and a double helix drawn with black eyeliner stabbed her forehead. She had a vaguely Egyptian look, and favoured the South American writers, although she already feared they were becoming passé. She despised alliteration, coordinated colours, synthetic zari, Dubai expatriates and Gulshan Kumar's bhajans.

Vatsala worked with an advertising agency. She had done a stint in Bombay before settling down in Delhi where, alas, the scene was not 'professional'. She had faced heartbreak thrice, twice in Bombay and once in Hissar, where she had lost her heart to a dairy farmer. Vatsala had gone to Hissar to get the feel of the place for a new account. The dairy farmer was a consultant to a new

Indo–Danish collaboration, and she had succumbed to his manly charms amidst the mooing of cows and malodorous whiffs of manure.

But nothing came of it. Back in Delhi, life continued as before. It took half an hour in a sputtering auto-rickshaw to get to her office in Connaught Place, sometimes even forty-five minutes. She retraced the same route across the Ring Road in the evenings, through the dull Delhi dusk. She had sold her olive-green Maruti 800, bought on a Citibank loan, after a rogue tempo had run amok and repeatedly rammed into its defenceless body as it stood parked outside her ground-floor Vasant Kunj flat.

The flat was pleasingly done up in muted shades and natural fabrics. Vatsala had a small study, where the pixels on her monitor flickered into the late hours of the night. 'Thus shone the lonely light in Milton's tower,' she murmured to herself, as she laboured away at the verse drama in eighty-four stanzas with which she hoped someday to stagger the world.

She would then retire to her quiet air-conditioned bedroom, where photographs of her nieces and nephews hung next to the bathroom door, and a poster for a bullfight which she had picked up during a holiday in Spain was pasted on the wall above her bed.

The guest room, done up in anaemic pastels, was reserved for her family. When Vatsala's parents came down from Dehradun, she felt a bit cramped, but dutifully put up with everything, even the familiar programmed remonstrations about finding herself a nice boy soon.

At the age of thirty-five, when her firm conical breasts had mysteriously enlarged from 34B to 36C, Vatsala Vidyarthi suffered a spiritual crisis. It began with a nagging question. 'To what purpose?' she would ponder, as the auto-rickshaw trundled through the traffic, past the outstretched hands of beggars with their babies-in-arms, through the familiar tired tenements of our country's capital, until the gracious arches of Lutyens's folly welcomed her back to work.

'Whatever for?' she would ask aloud, as she scanned the agonizingly cute copy for yet another brand of baby food. As she left the office in the evenings, the mandatory black coffee still bitter in her mouth, she would resolve to find a good chartered bus that suited her timings. Again, the tired traffic, snaking across the congested arteries of the Ring Road until the Qutab Minar, lit by powerful strobes, its phallic lines cutting across the comatose sky, shook her back to the immediate concerns of existence.

They were: fresh bread and eggs, lonely nights, power cuts, the search for a good drycleaner, and the subconscious reaching out for another presence as she held her pillow through the long lonely night.

You might exclaim that this is merely common or sparrow angst, the city-dweller's ennui. Those of you with

67

a humbler vocabulary may even bluntly call it loneliness, or ascribe it, in the fashion of the times, to the ever-worsening pollution in our cities. But no, Vatsala knew there was more to it, she was searching for something and, having worked in Bombay, and priding herself on being a professional, she knew she would not rest until she had found it.

Now, Vatsala Vidyarthi was a literal lady. To search, as in to quest, to seek, to look, to find, became a pitiless exercise in self-discipline and logistics. She took up yoga, and woke at dawn to contort herself mercilessly before setting out for her office. She joined a pottery class in Garhi village, taking time off from the agency to shape damp clay into function and meaning. She took up good works: registering with an NGO to counsel late-night suicide calls. But no one called, and she had the sensitivity to see that her pottery was ungainly, and the yoga made her irritable and exacerbated her sinus.

The agency experienced a mild upheaval when her boss left, along with four colleagues, to start an advertising firm of his own. He was replaced—so swiftly that it might have been providential, by a live-wire Madrasi with a thing about the rural market. Mr Raman, 'Manny' to his friends, was a hyperactive, hyperbolic wog with an unerring ear for punchlines. Before she knew what was happening, Vatsala was packed off to the Kumbh Mela (about which she later wrote a piece for *A&M*). New accounts were pouring in, and Manny instructed everyone in the agency to subscribe to at least one vernacular newspaper or magazine, in the language of their choice, to keep in touch with the masses.

Vatsala's odyssey to the real India began to tell on her copy. She wowed one and all with her artful espousal of Dunkel (sponsored by a progressive multinational) on behalf of DRAG, which, as everyone knows, is the Directorate for Research on Agriculture. A simple smudge of kumkum replaced the ornate artwork of the double helix bindi, and she regretfully bid adieu to salads after the rural E Coli bacillus played havoc with her digestion. She decided that nail varnish did not let her toenails breathe, and even contemplated letting her 36C breasts out of the unnatural restraint of an underwired bra. But that would be rash, keeping in mind the turbulent daily auto-rickshaw rides on Delhi's potholed streets. She decided, regretfully, to settle for a colourful ghagra-choli on weekends.

Vatsala Vidyarthi was an Indian lady, and when she was dispatched to Rishikesh on a recce trip for a new account for which Manny was gunning, she went with a distinct sense of piety and reverence.

The product was a dual-purpose herbal incense-cum-mosquito mat, to be christened after the holiest river in India. The Ganges, which had already endorsed products as diverse as soap and mineral water, remained for her the river of her childhood samskaras. After stopping for a night with her parents in Dehradun (her mother was down with the flu, her father's spondylitis was acting up again again), she left the next afternoon by taxi for the Ganges Riverside Retreat which, she had been assured, was a most suitable hostelry for a single unescorted lady.

Two things happened to Vatsala in Rishikesh. She found a man and, quite coincidentally, herself. Unrepelled by the mosquito mats of solitude and sadness with which she had surrounded herself, he came into her life, propelled, as it were, by pheromones.

He was a Slav, and although he was dressed all in saffron, he had the acrid manly smell of tobacco and sweat and meaty flesh. He strolled into her room by accident, mistaking it for his own. Vatsala had dutifully checked the safety latch before settling down for the night, but of course it didn't work.

She welcomed him in as an old friend. There was something disarming about the set of his eyes and the surprising purity of his face. He wore heavy mountaineering boots and a string of prayer beads around his neck. In his sturdy orange robes, he looked like a Buddhist monk returning from his travels.

They sat down together on the small balcony that overlooked the river, and listened peaceably to the steady sound of the water punctuating the silence of the night.

They might have been friends forever, so instant and complete was the understanding between them.

A cold mist rose like a wraith from the river, enveloping them in an odd intimacy. The stranger took out a cheroot from his voluminous rucksack. When the match burst into flame the tranquil contours of his face lit up for a brief second, and Vatsala longed to reach out and touch him.

'We cannot isolate mind from matter, nor separate the soul from the body,' he said, in a pleasantly accented voice, as he stripped off her nightshirt with clinical precision, and got to work with fanatical passion upon her body. Vatsala was so startled that she didn't protest at all, but gave herself up to the moment with feelings that bordered on detachment, if not resignation. The holy river, the early winter mist, the smoke from his cheroot that seemed to have penetrated her every crevice; she felt as though she were floating out of herself, escaping the confines of skin and nail and shampoo into a world of extraordinary immediacy. They sported together late into the night, until the stranger shuddered to a climax somewhere deep within her and, no, it was not as it had been with the married man or the dairy farmer.

'Now I am seeing for the first time, seeing directly without intervention of mortal eyes,' Vatsala said, only half to herself.

'I am him and he is me, we are in the river and the river is within us. There is a cosmic connectedness in it all. We are Yin and Yang, egg and yolk, Shiva and Shakti. I can, here in Rishikesh, transcend the barriers of time and space. Vasant Kunj was a dream, and the auto-rickshaw drivers, a nightmare. And even if this passion with a strange man is a sin, I can, after all, wash it all off in the Ganges tomorrow!'

The next morning she awoke with a body ache. She was alone, naked in her bed in the hotel room, without so much as a coverlet on her. The stranger, if he had come at all, had disappeared without a trace.

Vatsala put on some clothes and phoned room service for a cup of tea. The squat Garhwali waiter hung around stubbornly for a tip. It was only when she looked into her purse that she realized she had been robbed. No wallet, no watch, no money, except for some change scattered at the bottom of the purse. Even the credit card was gone. She scrambled around, willing it to be an absurd mistake, rummaging through the dirty clothes she had thrown into the cupboard.

The waiter shrugged insolently and left. The tea turned cold. She did not know quite how she could explain her predicament to the hotel or to the police. Wearily, she decided to call Manny at the agency. He would know what to do.

She couldn't get through to the operator. Vatsala sleepwalked to the front desk, where she was sure the

72

receptionist, who was covered in layers of artificial diamonds, gave her a knowing look. Summoning up all her self-possession, Vatsala gave her the number of the agency. She ordered another cup of tea for herself and waited for the call on the small deck that overlooked the sparkling waters of the river. A flight of steps led down to a private bathing area. Ancient, decomposing garlands of marigolds floundered around the black rocks.

The receptionist informed her that the line to Delhi was down. 'After all, this is UP,' she said consolingly. Vatsala felt so lost and alone that even this note of minor sympathy was enough to breach her defences. She found herself telling the receptionist that her wallet had been stolen.

'So why don't you call the police?' the receptionist asked, scratching her underarms as she spoke. Her cream-coloured blouse was stained with brown expanding circles of sweat. Vatsala realized anew that she was well and truly marooned.

'Actually, there was hardly any money in it,' she said hastily, but she was an ineffectual liar, and the receptionist arched her finely pencilled eyebrows in a manner that could have signified anything from scepticism to boredom. Vatsala affected an air of brave unconcern. 'I'm not the sort of person who bothers about money. The police can be such a bore,' she said, wishing, not for the first time, that she was better at untruths.

Since she wasn't sure about when she would be able to contact Manny or the agency, she decided to get down to work anyway. She resolved to walk so as to save money, and set off on foot towards the town.

Her brief was to scout for locations for Manny's new obsession, the Ganges Herbal range of incense-coated mosquito repellents. 'It's penetration we're looking for,' Manny had said, for the umpteenth time. 'The sex is in the volume. I want you to look around, soak in the atmosphere. We're marketing a concept along with a utility. It's important to understand the mindset of the base customer. Remember, he may be illiterate, but he's no fool.'

Armed with these wise axioms and dutifully equipped with a camera and a notepad, Vatsala set off. The town appeared dirty, and not particularly holy. The river seemed tantalizingly close. It could be glimpsed, glistening like a golden ribbon, between the shanty-shops and diesel trucks that lined the road.

Vatsala was tired, her head ached and her feet hurt. The dust tickled her sinus. She retraced her way to the Ganges Riverside Retreat and ordered herself a taxi. 'Put it on my bill,' she said with as much authority as she could muster.

It was a new diesel Ambassador. It worked. The driver was polite and courteous. When they hadn't run over man or dog by the time they reached Muni-ki-Reti, Vatsala decided that her luck must have changed.

'There is an air of eternity, even timelessness, about this place,' she noted mentally, when she saw the river again. But Vatsala detested clichés. Reproaching herself for visual laziness and a dependence on preconceptions, she set about re-examining the scene. The sunlight glinted joyously on the waters. There was a stillness in the air, a silence, removed from the noise of horns and the barking and the squealing of street dogs. The water was cleaner than she had imagined it would be. A sense of gladness descended over her like a benediction. 'Who am I?' she asked herself. 'And to what purpose?' but the old question stood shorn of tension and ambiguity. She even suspected that someone, somewhere, might know the answer.

A sadhu in a saffron loincloth was observing her intently. He was muscular and sinewy and his eyes were hard and observant. She felt herself blush under his gaze, and hurried on. Small children, bleached urchins with the sun in their eyes, sold her little polythene packs of fish food for the coins she could scrape from her purse. They ran away clutching the money she gave them, the sounds of their laughter only adding to the silence.

She was giddy with the sun and the heat and a strange, unfamiliar sense of elation. A ferry-boat slithered up right in front of her and, before she knew it, she had purchased an up-and-down ticket with her last few coins, and was halfway across the water.

The boat was full of people, people in polyester shirts and synthetic saris with zari borders, the great Indian masses. She looked at them curiously, searching for signs of commonality. 'Not that I feel superior,' she told herself hastily, 'it's just that our backgrounds are so different.'

The woman to her right, her face covered with a ghungat, threw some pellets of fish food into the river. Huge fish crowded by the prow of the boat, greedily gobbling up the brown pellets before they dissolved in the muddy water. They looked fat and grubby, obese and dissolute. 'They feed on flesh,' the woman on her right said shyly to no one in particular.

A rush of river air hit Vatsala in the face; it was an exhilarating bouquet of fish pong and iodine. She felt complete, liberated from her skin, forgetful of her many failures and recent humiliation. 'Is this an epiphany?' she wondered aloud, then reproached herself for dissecting everything.

Across the river, the atmosphere was different, more charged. Everything, from the ambling cows to the brass amulets piled up for sale by the riverbank, reeked of the sacred.

Vatsala Vidyarthi was a hardworking lady. She sat down by the steps of the bathing ghat and meticulously set about noting and tabulating her impressions. But the steep winding road, the Ram Nam chadars, the fragrance of marigolds—these images moved her to poetry and she decided to pen a freestyle haiku instead.

> The river flows
> On and on
> Even as the flowers
> Are caught in the eddies

And then decided it was not very original.

By now, she was feeling very hungry. The distinctive aroma of parathas frying on the griddle, bathed in real ghee (a smell she normally despised), lured her up a narrow lane. A fat man, fatter than a circus lady, dressed as a bahurupiya, simpered invitingly at his customers. A sign behind him proclaimed 'The one and only Chotiwala! Please try for taste.'

The idea came to her in the conventional shape of a bulb, a thousand-watt bulb. This was the perfect setting for their product. It would zap the rural psyche. Chotiwala endorsing Ganges Herbal Incense Mosquito Mats. It would give Manny a real rush.

Vatsala ordered herself a full meal, and gorged herself on aloo and puri and raita, rather like the grubby fish in the Ganges. 'They feed on flesh,' she said to herself reflectively. At the next table, a silent south Indian family was pensively contemplating a plate of vegetarian chow mein. When

Vatsala realized that she had no money she looked around her wildly, wondering what to do. The establishment did not look inclined to give credit. Perhaps the south Indian family might lend her some cash.

A male presence settled itself on the chair across hers. The acrid smell of marijuana clung to him like a blanket. He smiled at her from deep within his Slavic eyes, and companiably offered her a drag. Vatsala looked at him with shock and horror and revulsion. But when he touched her, a shiver rippled through her body. Fighting back her tears, she rushed out, weaving her way between the crowded tables until she was finally on the narrow lane outside. Something would not let her go and she found herself turning around, searching through the squeeze of customers. A ragged waiter was handing him her bill, along with a steel bowl containing a residue of aniseed and sugar. He took out his wallet and paid up with good grace, counting out the money in crisp new notes. An amused smile lit up his tranquil features. He was a detestable villain.

'At least the bastard paid for the meal,' Vatsala muttered to herself, wiping her eyes with the corner of her chunni. In the right light, the episode could even be viewed as funny. In fact, it was hilarious. She would tell Manny about it, and he would realize that she was not just a bluestocking, that she could be quite risqué when she so chose.

When she returned to the riverside resort there was another young woman, also draped in artificial diamonds, stationed at the reception. She handed Vatsala her room keys with an elegant sigh, then resumed the thoughtful scrutiny of her scarlet fingernails.

The room had been freshly sprayed with a powerful and malodorous insecticide. On the balcony lay hordes of delicate moths shuddering in their death throes. The sharp smell of the chemicals assaulted her larynx. 'What they need is some Ganges Herbal Incense Mosquito Mats,' she said to herself, quite loudly this time. It was becoming a habit.

She looked down at the Ganges. It looked no different from yesterday, the same damp river mist, the waters lapping at the shore, the steady rhythm of the mainstream. Across the river, a rectangular line of fires lit up the sparse forest cover. A corpse was burning merrily.

And we are here as on a darkling plain
Swept with confused alarms of struggle and flight,
Where ignorant armies clash by night.

Vatsala recited dreamily. For some reason, Matthew Arnold seemed particularly appropriate for the time and moment. The phone rang. It was Rita, the girl from the reception. 'We met in the morning,' she said. 'I have to speak to you.' It sounded serious.

She arrived at the door so quickly that Vatsala concluded that she must have telephoned from the next room. She was clutching her handbag, and fingering her fake diamond necklace with her shell-pink extremities. She was so excited that she practically fell into the room. 'I've recovered the money,' she said, emptying four thousand rupees in cash, two gold bangles and a credit card on to the double bed that straddled the room. 'It was the waiter! I don't know how he managed to get in! Perhaps you forgot to lock the door or you were bathing?'

Vatsala remembered that she had been quite naked when she awoke, without even the benefit of a coverlet. She blushed, and stuttered her thanks.

'The management has already fired him,' the voluble Rita continued. 'I always suspected that there was something wrong with him. I'm very sensitive, you know. I think you'll agree that we needn't call the police.'

Vatsala wondered what his name was and if she would ever find out. He had made love to her, and he had paid for her lunch. Vatsala Vidyarthi was a lady, and she wondered at her own behaviour.

'I think I'll return to Delhi now,' she said faintly. Before she knew it, she had paid the bill, and was bundled into an Ambassador car, a ramshackle one this time. She debated about whether to stop over in Dehradun and visit her parents, but decided against it.

Vatsala Vidyarthi was a real lady, and decided to keep the incident to herself. Whenever she remembered it, she felt a deep sense of regret, followed by an inordinate sense of relief. Sometimes, she would sigh when she scanned a page of particularly tedious copy or penned a haiku or read a poem by Matthew Arnold.

'Perhaps . . .' she would think, 'who knows!'

A short story is supposed to snap shut at the end with a sort of satisfactory click, but it would be difficult to distort this tale to fit an artistic requirement. My quarrel with the short story is precisely that it imposes a false order and symmetry on events, forcing impressionable young minds to anticipate a similar state from the inchoate mess that is life.

Even Manny agreed in the course of an abstract discussion that a punchline is not always essential to a good denouement.

Kunti

All my sons loved me, in their different ways. Yudhisthira, seed of Dharma, the god of righteousness, was born on the eighth hour of the day, when the moon was in conjunction with the constellation of Abhijit. My second son, Yudhisthira, eldest of the Pandavas, embodiment of virtue. Mighty-armed Bhima, born of the wind god Vayu, fell from my lap the day he was born, shattering into a hundred fragments the hilltop where I was resting. I remember the day well: it was the day Gandhari gave birth to Duryodhana.

Yudhisthira's virtue, Bhima's strength. Then, my valorous son Arjuna, the brave and invincible seed of Indra. I loved him the most. My sons Nakula and Sahadeva, brave, righteous and beautiful, born of the immortal Ashwins from the womb of my co-wife Madri.

I have known the love of gods and divine beings—five of them. Durvasa's bitter blessing brought glory to Pandu's line. But I never knew the love of my husband. He never fondled my breasts or stoked my joys in the conjugal bed. It was Madri after whom he lusted, always, with his impotent body and hungry spirit. I was his lawful wife, but all he wanted from me was heirs, kings to wear the crowns of conquest, warriors to sacrifice in battle.

'Go to a learned brahmana,' he would say. 'There is no sin in seeking out a rishi and requesting him to interrupt his austerities. No, I shall not be jealous.'

I told him of the boon that Durvasa had granted me. His eyes slanted with surprise, with subverted lust. Together, we summoned the gods, one after the other, and I took their seed. But I never told Pandu of how, when I was young, the Sun god had shown me his radiance and I had belonged to him alone.

*

I look back on that time when I was a young girl as though it were a dream. That girl who was then me.

'My beloved Pritha,' my birth mother would murmur, holding me close to her breasts, overflowing with milk. Even as I reached out to suckle, I was handed away, pushed to the wet nurse. Sweaty, comforting, maternal, she was, unlike my mother, not the sport of kings.

My mother was obsessed with her figure, with the need to stay slim and shapely at any cost. The palace was full of ambitious women casting their eyes at my father, the king Prithibhoja. After every war and skirmish, princesses would be heaped on the palace, trophies of victory, pledges of fearful alliances. It was but natural that my mother should be careful to maintain her beauty, and that she named me Pritha to remind him of their union. My brother was named Vasudeva, a name befitting the future king of the Vrishnis.

Daughters were dispensable: between the fathers and the husbands and the sons, their status was always in flux. Just a year after my birth, I was gifted to my father's cousin Kuntibhoja, as casually as I had been handed over to the wet nurse by my mother. My name was changed as well; I became Kunti, in honour of my new father.

It grieved me that my parents had given me away. I worked hard to earn the love of my foster-parents. Always smiling, full of wise words, even as a child, I became famous for my forbearance. I treasured every nod of approval. If a dog wagged its tail at me, I was grateful for the attention.

At the time of my puberty rites, my birth mother sent me a set of blue and red garments, of soft billowing moonga silk. My adoptive father Kuntibhoja gave me a set of twelve gold bangles, which the river goddess Sona in the northern mountains had gifted to our ancestors.

'Remember, my daughter, that gold becomes purer by the test of fire,' my foster-father said, as he fitted his gift on my wrists. I smiled, pleased, eager to demonstrate my gratitude. I made a resolution, 'I shall submit myself to every test with fortitude,' even as I admired the pure sheen of the bangles.

The rishi Durvasa was to visit our kingdom. The guest from hell. Everyone was in a state of panic, for Durvasa's irrational rages and irascible curses, irrevocable because of his penances, wreaked regular devastation upon his hosts.

'Kunti will attend on the rishi,' my foster-mother declared, a look of deep satisfaction breaking through her normally impenetrable face. I did not then understand that look, I was only grateful for being chosen for such a difficult task. I oversaw the appointment of the guest quarters, flowers in bowls, clean sheets. The bathing pool was scrubbed and scattered with lotus blooms. My preparations were thorough.

Durvasa was an easy guest, not bad-tempered at all. 'I cannot suffer fools,' he said, twinkling at me conspiratorially. 'Every king and prince I meet begs for a boon: Give me more kingdoms! Grant me a son! Gift me immortality! My bad temper keeps them away, and if they persist, I pack them off with a curse as recompense.'

'Such are the ways of kings,' I replied, as neutrally as I could, and with the modesty for which I was already famous.

Durvasa was pleased. 'What a sensible young lady we have here!' he exclaimed. 'I think you deserve a boon. What is it you would choose? Beauty, fame, wisdom?'

'Whatever you feel a young girl would most enjoy,' I replied demurely, adjusting my billowing red and blue skirts.

'The very gods shall be at your command,' Durvasa declared, his dark eyes flashing with mischief. 'With the divine magic of this mantra that I now reveal to you, every god and deva from the world beyond shall come to you at your desire, and live on in your bloodline by gifting you his seed.'

'What if I forget the words of the mantra?' I asked anxiously. 'I am only a mortal.'

Durvasa placed his hands on my forehead. His bony knobbly fingers pressed down hard on my skull, so hard that I bit my lips and drew blood. The sacred beeja, the sounds of intent of the mantra, coursed through my body like a revelation, even as the rusty taste of fresh blood filled my mouth.

'We rishis have no need of words, dear child,' Durvasa

said, as he removed his hands. 'Do not tell your father or your foster-father of my gift. No one from this palace should know anything of it, or they will try to wrest it from you for their advantage. Carry your courage as proudly as your beauty; in wisdom, you will never be found wanting.'

That evening, he strode away from the palace grounds, waving his brass kamandala, carrying away the whiff of forest that his bark robes had brought into the perfumed chambers of the guest quarters.

The king commended me for handling him so well. 'The head gardener claims he saw Durvasa smile,' he said. 'Kunti, you have served our kingdom well.' He was sitting on his throne, his consorts beside him, and the usual gaggle of courtiers and hangers-on in attendance. The chief queen looked sour and said nothing.

Durvasa's visit changed something in me. I no longer felt the need to please people. 'Carry your courage as proudly as your beauty,' he had said to me. I began to walk differently, with my head held high. The women in the palace noticed the change in my demeanour, and observed that it was time I was married off. Durvasa's secret mantra had changed my life.

I, too, was restless for change. I would not sleep all night, only sigh and long for things I could not understand. All night, I heard the river murmuring seductively by my window. Bathed in moonlight, I would watch the waves playing on the sands of the river Yamuna. She was the river of destiny for our Vrishni clan, our kingdoms flourished by her whims. She gave us floods and brought riches to our soil. Yamuna gave us trade, and when the waters dried up and the river serpents crawled on to the land, we prayed for her forgiveness.

The sky had remained sullen all through that monsoon. It had rained and drizzled for days on end. I had grown weary of the half-light, and my eyes had tired of the unvarying expanse of green earth and gray sky outside my window.

'How I wish the Sun would appear!' I sighed. Just for practice, I went through the mantra that Durvasa had imparted to me. The sounds of the invocation fell into place, vowels following consonants in sonorous ritual order. In that moment, in the private quarters of the palace, curtained from the world, a soft light like the first break of dawn filled up the room. I could sense him beside me, and then, in a blinding flash of fulfilling glory, I saw Surya, the god who brings the three worlds to light.

My eyes were dazzled. I saw him, not with my sight, but with every pore of my being. The light spread and became a low humming sound. Even as I drowned in that ocean of incandescent burning, the god surged and swelled inside me. His lips on mine as tongues of fire devoured my throat. His seed a burst of life, growing and coming to light. My womb contracted, first with joy and then with pain. My eyes were closed but I saw the glory of a thousand suns. The god departed.

Outside, I could hear the rain beating steadily on the flagged stones in the central courtyard. There was thunder and a bolt of lightning filled up the room. The silver streaks illumined the face of the child emerging through my parted legs. He examined me with steady eyes, liquid with trust. Karna, born of my words, seed of Arka whom I had invoked with the magic of Durvasa's boon. The infant wore his father's gifts of an invincible armour and a golden helmet. Gold kundalas hung from his ears, nestling among the radiant curls that betrayed his divine lineage.

And I, a mortal, was afraid. What explanation would I give the king and his consorts? What sort of a boon was this?

My son whimpered for milk, and I was glad that the beating rain masked his cries. My budding breasts swelled as I fed him, my young nipples hurting as he sucked, greedily, then contentedly, before he fell asleep.

I placed him in the reed basket that housed my ragged childhood dolls. Then I went to the courtyard and plucked some lotus leaves from the pond. The fish rose to nibble my fingers as I broke the mossy stems, one by one, and wiped them on my skirts. It had stopped raining but the sky was still overcast, swollen with the promise of more heavenly tears. I covered my son with the lotus leaves, to protect him from the rain. Then I swaddled him gently in a scarf of orange silk, and walked with light steps to the riverbank. No one, not the royal consorts, nor the handmaidens, would guess my sorrow or my intent from my gait, my demeanor. To them, I was a child still.

I hid behind a bush when I saw the court jester walking moodily along the slushy path to the riverfront. Laughter was his occupation, his duty, but oft-times, he would scowl and growl, then turn unexpectedly gentle. I waited until he had passed and placed the basket with my son in a bank of reeds by the river.

My birth father had named me Pritha. Then, when it was expedient for him to send me away, he had gifted me, as if I were a basket of freshly picked fruit, to his cousin and ally Kuntibhoja. I became Kunti. I became someone who could call the gods. The secret mysteries of dharma are full of summonings and partings.

The sound of distant thunder. The waters were rising steadily. I wept, but the tears did not lighten my heart. The little boat on which I had set my child afloat broke loose of the reeds. It danced joyously with the river currents, and the Yamuna, that sacred and kind-hearted lady, bore him away to his destiny.

I know today that Adiratha the charioteer discovered the basket as it floated down the river. He rescued my son, and with his wife Radha reared him as their own.

It is a curse to be born a kshatriya. All this talk of honour and duty; whose honour is it? Whose duty? I had borne the seed of the Sun god. My son Karna was noble, brave and generous. Yet I killed him. Once, and then again. Whose honour? Whose duty? It was simply fear of being found disobedient, of disgrace.

*

All my sons loved me, and I loved them all. Arjuna belonged to my heart in a way I cannot explain. But of all that I have loved and lost, my son Karna is the foremost. I see him every morning, in the reflection of the sun, in the dewdrops that glisten on the leaves.

It was because I loved him the most that I betrayed him. In my mother's heart, I had that right. When, deep into the days of battle, I met Karna and declared our blood bond, I asked him for the gift of Arjuna's life. With the generosity of the sun who gives us life and nourishes all, Karna granted me my wish. He gave everything away—his armour, his life. It is not Karna's forgiveness that I seek; he gave me that when I reclaimed him, to ask him not to fight his brother Arjuna in battle. It is not my own forgiveness, for I will never grant it. I seek the mercy of my son's father. The god who filled me with radiance and granted me a son who was the greatest warrior ever born. I seek his mercy to redeem me from the sins and sorrows I bestowed on my firstborn.

We sit together in a grove of pine trees, Gandhari and I. We have lost our kingdoms, though my sons rule Hastinapura still. Dhritarashtra and Vidura have gone for a walk in the forest, Vidura leading his aged, defeated brother, as spiritually blind as he is physically unable to see, through the unseen glories of the blooming kadamba trees. Gandhari is muttering to herself, as usual. The bandage around her eyes is grimy. Here, in our mountain retreat, we do not have servants to do our bidding. I shall wash the bandage in the stream tomorrow.

In a sing-song voice, the queen is intoning the names of her hundred slaughtered sons. She begins, as usual, with the eldest, in the order of birth. Gandhari can weep and mourn her hundred sons, because she did not kill them. I dare not lament for Karna, even now, except with the scorched, secret tears of shame when I see the first rays of the morning reflected on the dewdrops.

As Gandhari mutters and sighs for her hundred sons, I remain dry-eyed. It is high noon, and the rays of the sun warm my back in benediction. I was weak when I should have been strong, afraid of Kuntibhoja and his sour-faced chief queen. And when the time came to weigh my duty to myself or to the Pandava clan, I chose but the empty compulsion of duty. Not the memory of joy.

Love's Mausoleum

The streets of Delhi were a blurred green from the window of the car. At the crossing, a face materialized before me and, as is my habit in India, I shut my eyes. When I was young, my hand would reach for my handbag, but of late, I've changed. I look away. It's important to avoid eye contact. They know every trick, these people, and as the young man's bony fingers banged against the secure glass barrier of my brother's black Mercedes, I looked determinedly away until the lights changed and the car sped off, the well-trained chauffeur maintaining his mask of pleasant indifference. The beggar, miscalculating both his own guile and my vulnerability, was thrown off balance by the motion of the powerful car. His worn wooden crutch splashed in the monsoon slush, and resignation flooded his face. I could not shut my eyes completely. No one ever can—the eyes register, the ears register, even if the mind resists. The beggar shrugged his shoulders—it was a manly shrug, there was no spite in it—and then he approached the next lot of cars.

India is full of poor people, we can't feed them all, it is the government's job to do something. That's what we pay taxes for. That's what my brother always says, and my husband . . . my ex-husband now, his views were really no different.

As for me, I've learnt to look away, I learnt that early on in my marriage. My mother-in-law explained it to me, very long ago, when I was still in India. 'Men are like that,' she had said. 'They are different. You have to learn to shut your eyes. But remember, you are his wife, and nothing can ever change that.'

That's what she said, but she has been dead almost six years now; her diamond ring glitters on my finger, and my husband and I, we are divorced.

I had thought the worst was over in our marriage. I had looked away, I had ignored his indiscretions, forgiven his vulgarities, absolved him of his infidelities. I had been certain that, in his way, he continued to love me, or at least care for me. The divorce took me completely by surprise, although he did make a very generous settlement, and anyway, money was not the problem, it never has been. Perhaps that was one of the problems between us.

Because, face it, women find rich men attractive, and my husband—my ex-husband now—is so very rich that they flocked to him like flies to halwa. He loved their attention. I looked away as long as I could, but Sheila was more persistent than the rest, she persuaded him that they were in love. Ramesh—that's my husband—he's very gullible really, and, eleven years after we married, six years after my mother-in-law's death, we were divorced, and I was on my own, here in Delhi, in my brother's guest house.

I grew up in Bombay—my brother lives there still. I haven't really decided where I want to live, or what I want to do next. It's a relief that I'm childless. Children would have complicated things, though, perhaps, Ramesh wouldn't have left me if I had had them. It's really his sperm count—the doctor told me that, but he'll never admit it. And that Sheila, I know she played on his feelings. 'It's not as though you have children, Ramesh,' she told him (my brother had his telephone tapped), 'it would have been different if there were children. There's nothing to hold you together, you're not really a family at all.'

The car sped to the airport, where I was going to receive my friend Amanda, who was coming from London to see the Taj Mahal. She was meeting up with some friends in Dharamsala after that. Amanda and I don't have much to say to each other. I'm shy with people, but I like Amanda and am comfortable in our silences. And so the next day saw us on the highway, on the Mathura road, past all that industrial-looking construction and the screech of traffic noises which even the well-behaved purr of the Mercedes could not hide.

I've always loved the Taj Mahal. It's the most romantic building in the world. I mean, think about it: which other man would spend twenty-two years of his life and all that money on his wife? It always makes me want to cry. I wish I could be loved like that.

The landscape was very pretty—cows and camels, and flooded fields mirroring the monsoon skies. Amanda stopped once or twice to take photographs, and then, after Mathura, she wanted to stop at a dhaba for a cup of tea. I tried to explain to her how it was not really safe; how those truck drivers go mad when they see a white woman, we could both get raped, but she wouldn't take no for an answer. And then, of course, she had to take photographs of the truck drivers, those huge sardarjis lying on their khats and charpoys, scratching their crotches. I hear they've all got AIDS.

The hotel was a relief. That's what I'm used to: marble lobbies, soft carpets, the safe smell of affluence. My husband Ramesh always said he operated best in a 'controlled environment'. I think I do, too.

We decided to visit the Taj at sunrise. It's always most beautiful at dawn, wrapped in the morning mist. Besides, they have special entry fees and it costs more then, which one doesn't really mind because then you don't have the janta pouring in.

I've always felt so sorry for poor Mumtaz Mahal. I mean, imagine after having been the consort of Shah Jahan, the chief wife of the emperor, the light of the Mughal court, to now have your tomb swarmed over by all those Bihari labourers. She must be turning in her grave, literally. Of course, the real graves are underground, but I think they let the public in. I remember going to the Taj on a Friday once—the entry is free on Fridays—there were all those crowds, and everything stank of death and poverty. All those old women from Maharashtra in their nav-vari saris—they all resembled Gangubai who cleans and swabs in our Bombay flat—were staring in astonishment, in amazement, at the Taj. I guess they'd never seen anything like it before.

Amanda, too, was amazed. I've seen that with foreigners, they're always unprepared for the beauty of the Taj. The photographs never quite prepare one for the amazing harmony, the graciousness of the proportions—everything is just as it should be. It could never have been any other way. And the Yamuna, swollen by the monsoons, flowing beside the Taj, a river of silk in the gentle morning light.

They say that Shah Jahan was going to build another Taj Mahal, a contrast in black marble, across the river on the opposite bank. I'm glad he didn't, that his son Aurangzeb stopped him. I think it would have looked a bit like a chessboard. Perhaps I'm wrong.

I wonder if she had been good in bed—Mumtaz Mahal Al Zamani. (I always topped in history in my boarding school in the hills). She had married him when she was twenty. He hadn't looked at another woman after that, or so they said, and she had died delivering her fourteenth child. Seven living children, seven dead, in twenty years. She must have been perpetually pregnant—pregnant or nursing. Of course, she wouldn't have nursed her children herself, they had wet nurses for that.

I wonder about her sex life, whether she ever had an orgasm. I've never had an orgasm in my life—we were never good in bed together, Ramesh and I. And, of course, there was never anybody else. After all, I'm an Indian woman, aren't I?

Things might have been different if we had children, though, look at Shah Jahan, if you please, seven children from his favourite wife, and what do they do? Aurangzeb, the youngest, murders Dara Shikoh, the favourite son, and then imprisons his father in Agra Fort. I can just imagine Aurangzeb, he must have been a righteous sort of man, like my brother, perhaps. He must have hated Shah

Jahan's extravagance, for the Taj Mahal must have cost a pile, surely.

I remember reading somewhere that when Aurangzeb wanted to borrow Shah Jahan's jewels for his coronation, the old man got so incensed that he began pounding the priceless gems into dust with a mortar and pestle. It was his eldest daughter Jahanara Begum who stopped him. Begum Sahiba, I think she was called.

I read in the same book that Shah Jahan slept with her, after her mother died. 'He ate the fruit of his own bough,' was how contemporary historians described it. He must have been very lonely after Mumtaz Mahal died and, perhaps, Jahanara Begum had looked like her mother. Anyway, it sounded inexcusable, but I guess the rules are different for emperors.

Amanda flitted about with her camera. She was clearly enjoying herself, swooping through the white marble in her black cape and tights, looking like an agitated bat. 'There can never be another Taj Mahal, can there, Malika?' she exclaimed, rolling her eyes the way she does. I told her how Shah Jahan had had all the craftsmen maimed and disabled by imperial decree, so that they would not be able to build a rival palace for any monarch anywhere else. I always enjoy telling foreigners that story. I love to see how disconcerted they get; they look horrified, they never know quite how to react.

All this while, we were being accosted by touts and guides and photographers who offered to show us around, but we dexterously avoided them. The rain had washed the marble clean and it looked young and translucent. When the clouds parted and the morning sun lit the marble that reflected the light from the river, I held my breath in wonder. Beauty is such a puzzle, it always has the capacity to take you unawares, again and again.

I used to be considered beautiful when I was younger, even Ramesh had been crazy about me, but although I look much the same even now—my figure is still good, and so is my skin—something has changed. I'm an objective person, and I know that. I look stressed, burnt out, as well I might. Indian marriages are not supposed to break up the way mine did.

The sun went behind a cloud, and a soft drizzle began to fall. Amanda squealed with delight, I have never heard her respond to the London rain like that. We went inside the cenotaph and, through the arched door, I observed the perfect symmetry of the water pavilions extending in an austere parallel to the noble domes of the main entrance. A guide attached himself to us, he wouldn't let us go and so, out of sheer inertia, we heard him through his pat discourse: about the twenty-two years it took to build the Taj; the twenty thousand workers; the engraved poppies on Shah Jahan's tomb; the echo in the dome, and so on. It was dark inside, and his torch kept sending beams through the darkness, lighting up an inlay, a flower, a geometrical design. There was a smell of death in the mausoleum. I knew that the real graves were safe in the actual crypt below; it was closed for repairs. This tomb of Shah Jahan and his consort Mumtaz Mahal was a dummy, built for symmetry, to distract attention from the real thing.

Amanda was suddenly whooping with delight again. I turned to find her in the arms of a very tall man, he looked like an American but when she introduced him, I discovered he was British like her.

'This is my friend Tony Rice,' Amanda said, and even in the darkness I could observe that her skin was glowing. 'What a marvellous surprise to meet him here!' They disappeared into the vaulted darkness with the guide, I could hear them oohing and aahing while examining the fretwork. Their enthusiasm made me very tired and I retreated to a corner and watched them do the rounds with the other tourists—the determined pink-skinned Germans, the Japanese, the T-shirted Indian NRIs.

When the rain finally stopped, we returned to the washed white marble outside. I saw a peacock atop one of the minarets, drying its plumage, flapping and shaking the great weight of its azure wings. For some reason, I did not point this out to Amanda and Tony—the bird was entitled to its privacy. Besides, they already had enough for their cameras.

And then, there was a squirrel, a small, fidgety squirrel, running up and down a neem tree, shaking its bushy tail dry of rain. When we passed though the forbidding main gates where the metal scanners and security outfits were stationed, I spotted two black kittens, their green eyes gleaming in the dark, sitting snug and dry in a nest of rolled-up coir matting.

The guide, who was still close at our heels, began chattering again in his peculiarly accented English. He pointed out the tomb of Shah Jahan's other two wives. He explained how they were buried outside the main complex because 'they were, both of them, unfortunately, barren and childless'. Commiseration oozed from his voice. I wanted to kick him in the crotch.

Tony accompanied us back to the hotel. Amanda wanted to rest for a while before lunch. Amanda is an attractive woman, but when we regrouped at lunchtime, she looked positively beautiful. 'Tony is going to Jey-pore,' she said, sounding as dizzy as a besotted teenager, 'and then to Uday-pore and Jod-pore. I've decided to go with him.' A breathless giggle escaped her. 'I'm afraid you'll have to return to Delhi alone, Malika.'

A cold feeling of spite was accumulating inside me, but I said nothing. The diamond on my finger, the one that had belonged to Ramesh's mother, glittered furiously, sending out sharp points of green and blue light. I studied it composedly, and tried not to listen to the badly sung ghazals which the hotel considered essential accompaniment to tandoori food.

The Indian food in London is much better than what you get in India—even Tony and Amanda said so. Although in my heart of hearts I agreed, I protested and said that what we were eating was not Indian food at all, not really. Suddenly, I remembered how the food my grandmother cooked used to taste. My grandmother was a Bengali, although she married a Sindhi. Her cooking was fragrant with flavours and redolent with the most unexpected spices. Just the memory of her fish curry made me want to weep, and I felt dreadfully lonely.

Agra is an ugly city, a hideous sprawl of dirt and grime, but, as we left its environs, I couldn't but fall into a romantic reverie about what the city must have been like in the time of the Mughals. I wondered if Sir James Roebuck was as silly and inconsequential as Tony Rice. I thought of the meena bazaars, where the women of the court used to display their wares for the king to examine. I wondered if they had worried about the lines under their eyes; about sagging breasts; about the loss of control. I saw myself, a court beauty, selling lacquered bangles and other baubles to courtiers and grandees, even the emperor himself.

Returning from Agra, alone, I looked out the misted windows at the galloping landscape. The drenched green earth looked contented and fulfilled, and even the chauffeur was smiling to himself and softly humming a song.

I remembered the time, very long ago, when I had often burst into song, spontaneously, without provocation. My mother thought I had a good voice—all mothers do—and I was dispatched to learn classical music from Ruma Devi, a blue-blooded aristocrat who had shocked her generation by learning thumris and dadras from the ladies of the night. Even her husband, a connoisseur of music, women and cigars, had drawn a polite line at her enthusiasm. But Ruma Devi took on an aged prostitute as her guru and, in time, her social circle learned to live with it, and even to appreciate her for her style and daring. That was, of course, a long time ago. I believe now it is the quite the reverse and every old nautanki singer is automatically elevated to the status of a Begum Akhtar by a society starved of excitement.

Anyway, I was remembering my childhood in a misty, idyllic kind of way, in keeping with the weather and the colours of the landscape when, suddenly, an unpleasant memory emerged with a little blip from the locked black trunk that constitutes my past. Every now and then, I just consign chunks of my life—the unpleasant parts—to this large trunk that sits improbably in the pastel drawing room of my head. It has a stout iron padlock, the key to which I have thrown away. But I know how to get it back whenever I need to lock things in. This was probably the first time in my life that something had tried to escape from the trunk on its own. I thought it was ominous, a bad sign, and I ignored the persistent image of the supple, monkey-like tabalchi who had been Ruma Devi's accompanist, the wizened, comical creature who rattled out dexterous beats on the two slightly askew tablas, and looked studiously appreciative, when Ruma Devi sang.

Ruma Devi had a way of looking at him, suddenly, in mid-song and he, too, would lift his eyebrows and nod his head and look even more appreciative than usual. I always found it very endearing. One day, when I was practising my scales, I gave him a similar look, I smiled into his eyes, and he lifted his head and nodded his eyebrows in reply. Ruma Devi was suddenly called away, there was a phone call for her, I think. The other students hadn't come that rainy day as the city was flooded. I lived nearby and my father's chauffeur had dropped me. In fact, he was waiting outside, and Ruma Devi was on the telephone, when the tabalchi leapt on me with a wild movement. His mouth was over mine, he was kissing me, inflicting upon me his dark tongue, his betel-stained teeth. I froze in fright, a seamless terror enveloping me so completely that even today, so many years later, I break out into a sweat at the very memory.

The image flickered in my mind for a fraction of a second, and then it was gone. I had blanked out the memory; I had forced myself to forget it again.

I tried desperately to remember what had happened. I drew a blank. I looked at the car, the chauffeur, the green outside, and I was confused about who and where I was. I could recall the fear, I was afraid of my father, I was afraid of being found out, I was afraid of becoming pregnant. I thought I might deliver a baby right there on the pot and since I wouldn't then have the heart to flush it away, my mother would find out what I had done.

Only today, umpteen years later, did it dawn on me with a flash—it was a flash, I swear, a flash of clean white light—that I had done nothing wrong. I was not guilty, I was not to blame, I had smiled innocently at Ruma Devi's tabalchi and he had attacked me, middle-aged beast that he was. And I forgave him, I am a generous person that way. I have forgiven my mother-in-law and my husband Ramesh for all the remembered and the forgotten atrocities. I forgave Furquat Khan for his unspeakable act. Most importantly, I forgave myself. Everything fell into place, my guilt, my fears, my silence, my hatred of my body. I knew suddenly what had gone wrong with me and Ramesh, why I had stopped singing.

Nowadays, they call it child abuse, I always found it a bit implausible, all those tedious newspaper articles and television interviews, all that exaggerated trauma, but now that my memory has dredged up that missing piece of the jigsaw, now that I remember what had happened, now that I have stumbled upon this important clue, it is as though the clouds have parted and let the sunlight in. This was what had initiated all the subsequent betrayals, and each consequent hurt had confirmed that first bitter assault.

It was my trust that had been abused, and once that first defence had been breached, the process had begun in earnest: my parents, giving me away like a piece of furniture; myself agreeing, always agreeing, the guilt gnawing at my insides, eating me up, until today, on my way back from Agra, a chauffeur's faltering song had released me from that imaginary prison, that forgotten past.

It's like that with me, everything happens very quickly. Now, with the speed of fluttering doves, that censored memory had escaped from the traps of the past. I'm not a poetic person, and I'm not making this up, but what happened next was sort of symbolic, it made me feel optimistic, somehow. We were still on the road to Delhi and, to the west, the sky had cleared, and a luminous rainbow was spread in a smiling arc over the horizon, its many colours shimmering against the pearly sky.

That's about as poetic as I'll allow myself to be. My family is Sindhi, remember, even though my grandmother was Bengali. I didn't burst into song, I didn't even smile, but the seven iron bands around my heart had snapped. The future lay as straight and easy as the road before me, and the past—well, it had fled. On the way back from Agra, I had left it behind somewhere on the road, with the Taj Mahal and all that.

The Day Princess Diana Died

'Every girl has a princess inside her,' my best friend in school would declare.

'Not me,' was my response, even then. 'I'm just on ugly stepsister.'

Sometimes, there are these stories trapped inside me, choking me as they seek articulation. They catch me by the throat and like a bawling baby, demand to be heard. You can see I'm getting my metaphors all mixed up. I often do that when I'm confused, which I usually am when I'm beginning to tell a story.

This is the story of a love affair, an old-fashioned love affair between two consenting heterosexuals that began with roses and rapture on a rainy day, when lightning streaked across a grey sky to illuminate the eyes of a long-lost friend. I had not met this man for almost a decade and yet, when we met again, the years just fell away and we settled back into the habit of being friends. It had been an easy, happy friendship, the sort that rarely develops into love; but this one did. Before you could say abracadabra, we were swearing never ever to leave each other, not to eat, breathe and survive, except together. We felt safe and fortunate, and my many girlfriends scattered through the city tuned in to my love-sick sighs with scorn or suspicion or sheer derision, depending upon their degree of sophistication and how many times their hearts had been broken.

I didn't notice these things at that time; I was too distracted by the special effects. We were in the mountains, in a forest rest-house together, soaked to the bone. We lit a bonfire of old packing cases and mouldy newspapers and some rather pretty pine cones. And, to the sound of the hissing flames and the orange glow that threw strange shadows on the wall, we made love for the first time, after so many years of knowing each other.

Of course, that changed things between us. I guess I should start telling this story better. I was back in Delhi by then, on a rather muggy monsoon morning. I remember that I was talking on the telephone, I forget about what or to whom, when my brother came into the room and switched the television on. 'Haven't you heard?' he asked.

'The princess is dead.' There was a blare of sound from the portable set that sits on my desk, and the girl on the screen lip-synced my brother's announcement. A mangled-up car that looked like a cockroach squashed by a pair of wooden clogs flashed on the screen, followed by a soft sob from my brother.

Although he's a lawyer and not in the least sentimental, my brother had wept repeatedly all through the four times he saw *Hum Aapke Hain Koun?* So, I decided not to console him, to leave it to time, the great healer. I'm not squeamish about death; I've seen a lot of it. Being a copy-writer, I couldn't help but congratulate the supreme scriptwriter on a masterly, if melodramatic, denouement. There was much to admire in a departure which had so much elan to it. To die young is to become immortal.

My brother had come for some toothpaste (for some reason, he's always running out of toothpaste, although he's never short of toilet paper). After he left, the maid came in to clean up the room. I was sipping my first wake-up cup of coffee when she settled down on the floor beside my bed and began one of her interminable conversations.

'It is the maharani of England who has died?' she asked me, squinting at the television set as she spoke.

'No, she was the rajkumari of England,' I replied.

'Why, wasn't she shadi-shuda, married-sharried?' she persisted.

'So she was,' I replied, wondering how to shut the woman up. She cleans well, but when she starts talking, she doesn't stop. 'But she had left the rajkumar, the prince . . .'

'She left her man? She had clothes, a house, some money, two sons, and that was not enough for her?' the cleaning lady inquired, grinding her supari into the corner of her mouth as she does when she's trying to make a point.

Downstairs, there was a deluge of tears. My father sighed and sniffled into his handkerchief, and then explained to nobody in particular that he was probably getting a viral. Perhaps, he mourned the loss of beauty, which is the most impenetrable of all mysteries. My mother wept more openly. She mourned the loss of youth, her own as much as anybody else's.

We had fixed up a girlie lunch that afternoon. A gaggle of girlfriends got together for a low-fat buffet at a new organic restaurant, and in the way that girlfriends have of being absolutely truthful when you don't want them to, they told me I was looking awful; what on earth had I been doing with myself? 'Your skin is looking sort of discoloured and puffy,' my best friend told me, 'and you've put on all that weight you'd lost.' I took this spate of compliments as gracefully as I could. I'm an ugly stepsister, not a princess.

The conversation turned, inevitably, to the car crash and the princess's death. 'Everybody dies,' I said, defiantly, smothering my fat-free salad with a cream dressing. This heresy was met with shocked looks and low whispers. My best friend's best friend who, quite naturally, is no best friend of mine, let out a low moan of pain and outrage. 'But she was the princess!' she squealed, and for the rest of the lunch, I was ostracized for my heartlessness. I tried to explain that the princess's constantly perfect good looks had rendered her unreal, if not surreal, in my eyes. 'You've got vinegar in your bloodstream!' my best friend replied.

It was when we were collectively paying the bill, searching in our purses for change and adjusting old IOUs, that my best friend's friend casually shattered my world. 'That handsome hunk you're seeing these days,' she said, casually, 'you'd better check him out a bit. I believe he lays out the broken marriage bit to every chick whom he chats up.'

The funny part was I didn't even know he was married. I have two marriages behind me: one ended in divorce, the other, in death. Now, I deduced the presence of a wife in the continuum of my lover's life, which rendered the perfect circle of our love into a potentially unappetizing triangle. I remember how it felt, to be left for someone else—was I charting those troubled waters again?

In the office the next day, all the girls were in mourning, and the men, in different degrees of shock and utter devastation. 'Really!' the girl at the reception said, articulating the voice of many like the chorus in a Greek tragedy, 'Really, some people have no feelings!' She was referring to my refusal to mourn. I tried to explain that my own life was getting a bit complicated. To which she responded by lifting an eyebrow.

The liftman in our building had died, but that didn't seem to bother anybody. And when I suggested we take out a collection for his family, the idea met with frosty silence. I guess the deaths of the poor and the aged inspire little grief, while the death of the young and beautiful is the death of dreams. So, no tears for the liftman.

I must explain our office is not into cricket or football or things like that. The indigenous sport on the eighth floor of Kailash Towers, in the ad agency where I work, has been, for some months now, the scoring of an elaborate battle between the Royalists and the Loyalists. The Royalists, who thought Prince Charles was in the right, were, from the very beginning, in a hopeless minority; they were, I suspect, contrarian by nature. Furthermore, one of them claimed to be Nirad Chaudhuri's nephew. The Loyalists believed in blue blood and bulimia and Barbara Cartland, and they were vociferous in their arguments and they always won.

The camps were mixed up today, with the monarchists confusedly weeping for Dodi Fayed. The serial melodrama of the princess's life had the social snobs and the celebrity snobs all mixed up.

I had always claimed neutrality, refusing to take the sport seriously. Didn't I have enough problems of my own? I am not good-looking, and have always hated beautiful women. They are vain, difficult, selfish, and yet, somehow, they always manage to have it all. I bet my first husband wouldn't have left me if I had been a bit easier on the eye. Frankly, I couldn't understand why Anand (the man with whom I was in love), found me irresistible. 'It's something about your eyes,' he told me, enough times by now so that I was tempted to believe him.

I was to have dinner with my lover that night, the night of the day Princess Diana died. We ate dinner at a new Italian restaurant and drank a lot of wine. I confess I was a bit wobbly when I walked out. We went for a drive later, and were pottering about aimlessly for a while when I confronted him about his marital status. 'We're not really together anymore,' he said, after a second's hesitation. 'You could say we were never really together,' he continued, after a few more minutes of careful consideration. 'She doesn't understand me, she can't fathom my needs.' A wave of nausea rose within me, I wasn't sure if it was the food or what he was saying. Then, we went back to his flat and made the most perfect love. Post-coital sadness is all very well, but after he had lit a cigarette and flushed away the condom, Anand switched on the television set and burst into tears. 'She was the only woman I ever really loved,' he sobbed, 'and now she's dead!'

'I always found her too beautiful to be real,' I said, 'perhaps I was just jealous. It must be wonderful to be so perfect.'

'The man was a swine,' he continued, 'how could he betray her like that?'

'Which man?' I wondered, but not aloud. Then I asked him if he had loved his wife, and he said no, then yes, and then made it sound like a maybe.

'She's a kind-hearted woman, she has been weeping all day for Princess Diana . . .'

Well, I won't give you a blow-by-blow account, but this escalated into the most dreadful fight. And I refused his offer of a lift and phoned the taxi stand for a black-and-yellow cab, which sputtered with indignation all the way home.

At home, in the safety of my own bed, I made a resolution. I would never ever fall in love again. Having made the resolution, I had a banana and a glass of warm milk and got into bed.

The television channels were still going on about her. There was a talk show centred around a press photograph of the Princess of Wales seated alone on a marble bench in front of the Taj Mahal. She had visited the mausoleum of love in 1992, on a state visit.

'I would interpret the photograph as a statement of solitude,' the spectacled lady psychoanalyst on screen pronounced authoritatively.

People who believe in love stories rarely know how to love. It's like a sugar addiction or something. In the strange half-tones between dozing and sleeplessness, I realized there had been a princess inside me, too. Everybody has a fairy tale in them, waiting to be betrayed.

Grand Hotel III

Outside the open window, in the square, the clip-clop of horse's hooves. The Grand Hotel Krakow is kind, gracious and discreetly faded. It has taken me in, after months of international travel and inhospitable airports, like an old aunt who has dealt with generations of difficult kin.

It's been a bad year, unrelentingly depressing. My father died, my husband divorced me, my Tibetan terrier succumbed to parvo virus. I got alopecia and chunks of hair fell out from my scalp for no reason at all. Other things happened, too, but I don't want to think about them just now. I rest my head, wrapped in a soft silk scarf, and listen to the sounds that float in from the open window.

There is a vase of flowers in the room, beautiful mauve lilies in a forest of dense ferns. Are they real? I get up to touch them, but it's no help at all. I can't tell, and smelling them is no use either, my nose is blocked, as are my ears, from all that travel. I take out the change from my wallet, the pouch is weighed down with pfennigs and pennies, and some zloty from the taxi ride. I can think of nothing, I understand nothing; I am a woman standing by a window in an unfamiliar hotel room, looking out. But it doesn't continue to remain unfamiliar, this room—it has begun to caress me, soothe me, take me in.

I think of all the Grand Hotels I have stayed in; summon memories of them; list them out. The Grand Hotel in Shimla, where a wandering monkey had once torn up my favourite pink frilly frock. I was six years old and the encounter left me inconsolable. The Oberoi Grand, when my lover and I had spent a night together, and my husband—now my ex-husband—had got to know. (His school friend was the general manager.) The room had a four-poster bed, the restaurant had excellent fish, and we had memorable sex. What had followed was abandonment, by my husband, by my lover. 'The Grand Dame of Chowringhee,' that's what my lover had called it. He was Bong, Bangla, Bengali. He still phones me sometimes. I don't miss him, he was baggage, but I miss my husband. Bad move.

I stayed in the Grand Hotel in Nuwara Eliya, on my honeymoon. It's a tropical Elizabethan manor house, where the smell of lemon grass and cinnamon pervaded our lovemaking. My husband, my ex-husband, had a moustache then, and it would tickle me in the strangest places.

Nuwara Eliya means Little England. The Governor of Ceylon, Sir something or the other, used to live there, in eighteen hundred and something or the other. It's history, all that, like my marriage. They had a flower garden with dahlias and hollyhocks and poppies, and a gardener who was madly proud of his 'Yinglish' garden. His name was Stanley, I remember. Maybe I'll go there again, sometime, to the Grand Hotel in Nuwara Eliya.

I want to return to the present, so I start Googling things compulsively. It's a harmless addiction—it makes me feel part of the world again.

The Grand Hotel has been ranked number 54 of 223 hotels in Krakow. It is described as 'discreet' and 'charming', and was once the residence of a Polish princess. The building, it seems, has been in existence from the second half of the nineteenth century. The Internet also says, 'Once in the hotel, you will easily forget the twenty-first century.' After the opening of the hotel in 1887, articles about the 'most luxurious and modern hotel' in Poland appeared in the press. I discover Joseph Conrad has stayed in the hotel.

I turn to Facebook. My ex-husband and erstwhile lover both like that I am in Krakow. My ex-husband's profile picture now includes a photo of his new girlfriend. She is short and dumpy and certainly less attractive than me. But then, he never had any taste, did he?

I slept. Good pillows. Grand dreams.

Most nights, I dream of lakes. I dreamt of the dried-up lake in Pushkar when I had been there with my husband—or was it my lover? It was confusing. And then, I was by another lake, in another dream—in the Pichhola Hotel in Udaipur, and the Café du Lac beside it, where I, in my dream, sat naked, caressing a drooping breast.

The next morning, I tested the pain, in my heart, in my breasts. It had not settled, but remained, like a grainy residue in my dry eyes.

I wore a business suit and shoes that pinched, and walked around the charming marketplace where the clatter of hooves reminded me of childhood holidays in Himalayan hill stations. I attended a meeting where my mind wandered, a meeting that ended with approving smiles and warm handshakes.

In the evening, a stranger in the hotel lobby suggested I go with him 'to the graveyard'. It was All Souls' Day, so that is why he had asked me. He wasn't a vampire or anything like that. He was a retired university professor from the US. His grandparents had lived in Krakow but they weren't buried in the graveyard which we visited. They died in Dachau or Auschwitz, he wasn't sure which. His wife had died too, that year, of breast cancer; but he wasn't grieving any more. Or so he said.

'I must go in for a mammography soon,' I told myself, as I often do.

We went together to the graveyard in a taxi. It wasn't that far away. It looked like Diwali, lights and flowers everywhere. No fireworks, of course. The stranger, his name was Franz, pointed out Conrad's father's tombstone. We examined the rugged wall of rough-hewn rock and nodded sombrely at each other.

'I have forgiven death,' Franz said to me, as we stood there surrounded by lights and flowers. 'Death and the imposters who think they are the agents of its perpetration.' He turned to me with an intense look and, by the flickering light of the lamps and candles, he looked strange, even crazed. A vampire?

I panicked, and found myself reciting a poem by Emily Dickinson:

Because I could not stop for Death,
He kindly stopped for me;
The carriage held but just ourselves
And Immortality.

It was his turn to look at me strangely. 'By Emily Dickinson,' I concluded, and things settled down between us after that. We had each other's measure—two lonely people in a graveyard on All Souls' Day.

We went for dinner to the Jewish quarter, to a deserted restaurant where I had pumpkin soup and Franz had— I forget what. In the hotel, by the lift, he gave me a peck on my cheek and his visiting card. Franz smelt musty but somewhere on his sleeve I caught the scent of lilies, of the flowers in the graveyard.

In the morning, I checked out and left for the airport. Changed flights twice. I was very tired, and forgot for a bit which airport I was at. They all look the same, and there are always Indians everywhere. Then I saw the girl with the bindi on her forehead, her hands folded into a decorously seductive namaste, guiding me into the ladies' washroom. The gigantic blown-up photograph reminded me I was at the new airport in Delhi. A city I once called home.

GIGALIBB

This one treads the slushy terrain between memory and fiction. I need to salvage at least something, a moral or a dictum or a wry smile, from those lived lives and remembered moments. There are still some persons alive whose sense of the past might be alerted, but then, of course, they might not ever read this story.

I hadn't met Kaka Kohli for almost ten years, when I encountered his photograph today in the obituaries section of *The Times of India*. It was a youthful likeness, in which he looked almost exactly as he had done when I first met him. I was seven, and my favourite aunt was getting married. Kaka had recently materialized in Nainital, and taken over the Metropole Hotel, which was locked in a deadly business rivalry with the Grand Hotel. Kaka Kohli had done the catering for my aunt's wedding. He had moved to our lakeside hill station from Bombay, where, it was rumoured, he had featured as the sidekick in a flop Hindi film. It wasn't Bollywood then, the word hadn't been invented, but I was extremely impressed.

At my aunt Bindu's wedding, after the guests had gone home and the waiters were wearily clattering the crockery around in the abandoned tennis field, Kaka Kohli had settled down on the broken concrete roller and burst into song. There were just a few of us around, no guests, only family, and we were not prepared for it, for the way in which his voice broke out of his chest and lifted up above the hill and across the lake, until it seemed to fill up sky and earth and cloud. I could imagine the bats flapping their capes to its lilting rhythm, the owls tapping their toes, the waves in the lake leaping this way and that in response. It rose with the low smoke that hung around the empty tandoor, rising and climbing up to the stars.

What was the song? I can't remember. But I haven't forgotten how it sounded and felt. It had to be a love song. It probably had words like 'prem' or 'ishq' in it, possibly 'mohabbat'. Kaka Kohli believed in love; it was, as he proclaimed, his religion.

'I am a prem pujari,' he would say, 'a priest of love. For God is great, and love is bloody blind . . .'

And that was what his obituary in *The Times of India* said: God is Great and Love is Blind. This was stated in bold italics over the black-and-white photograph, in the 'In Memoriam' section. Not 'Love is Bloody Blind', just 'Love is Blind'.

I was fourteen when I discovered that unexpected truth. I had developed an infatuation for a young man not distinguished for his intelligence. I offered my heart to him humbly, without hope of return. I had acne, and read poetry, and the boys I knew all enjoyed mocking me. I was naturally shy, and miserable about the way I looked, and the combination of circumstances led to cruelty, not teasing. The memory pierces as sharp as if it were yesterday.

There I am, standing by the steps of the municipal library by the edge of the lake, observing the ducks paddle past in happy camaraderie. The sky is blue, the sun shining, but my heart is weeping. I have witnessed the Man I Love walking into the local cinema hall with a Very Pretty Girl. Blinking away my tears, I stare even harder at the happy ducks.

Kaka Kohli is strolling past, waving an ivory walking stick. He stops to tell me a sardarji joke. It is about Santa and Banta and an aeroplane that doesn't take off but it doesn't even get me to smile.

Kaka's prem pujari radar is instantly alerted. 'You are such a lovely young lady,' he says, looking at me appreciatively with his grey eyes that squint ever so slightly.

'All the young men must be in love with you—and whoever isn't is just a fool. Because you see . . .' here he pauses, and adjusts his scarf this way and that, 'God is Great and Love is Bloody Blind.'

I experience a shift in perspective. The world seems suddenly all right again. The sky is still blue, the ducks are paddling in formation, still in the same direction. I can feel the happiness all around me and I am smiling.

Through my teenage years I continued to fall in love with desperate regularity. 'Love is Blind,' I would tell myself, through those times of hope and heartbreak. At age twenty-one, when I finally lost my virginity, age twenty-seven when at last I got married, forty, when I was more miserable than ever before, and at now forty-seven, as I confront Kaka Kohli on the obituary page, I have summoned that mystic mantra: 'God is Great and Love is Bloody Blind.' It encapsulates the highs and lows of life, and works as well as a large swig of whisky.

In a moment of inspiration, I got an antique silver pendant inscribed with the acronym GIGALIBB, which I would finger when in extreme distress.

Not that anyone thought of him as a philosopher. Kaka was a hotelier, a caterer, a slaughterer of chickens, a renter of rooms. Before that he had been an actor, which was even worse. He was reputed to have fallen in love repeatedly, sometimes with several women at the same time. As a local wit noted, it was his wife who seemed to be bloody blind about Kaka's loves.

Kaka was infatuated with my aunt, my mother's cousin, the one whose wedding party he had catered for. Bindu was blindingly beautiful; she looked like an inexplicable mixture of the actress Geeta Dutt and the venerable vamp Helen. She had a way of looking up heavenwards and exhaling a deep sad sigh that drove men mad. Being an observant and devoted niece, I had noticed this puzzling chemical reaction in process. It was compounded by the trick she had of letting her sari pallav drop. As the fabric slipped beguilingly off her shoulder, her small, perfectly sculpted breasts would come into view, while Aunty Bindu blushed and fell into an innocent confusion. She would look skywards and let out that deep sigh, then fumble prettily with her sari pallav until she had adjusted it demurely over her pale cleavage.

Once, on a school picnic to Kausani, I watched the clouds part to reveal a glistening Himalayan snow peak, then gather again to hide it up. It reminded me of my Bindu Aunty, and how she would cover up her breasts after her sari pallav had slipped down. Then the sun set, staining the sky pink like the blush on Bindu's face; I was quite pleased by the poetic conceit, and thought of committing it to rhyme.

My aunt Bindu was not a flirt. She was oblivious to the effect she had on men, and seemed surprised when they accosted her with protestations of love. Kaka Kohli, of course, never declared his love—it was outside the scope of his aspirations. He could clutch a lady rummy player's delicate wrist in the card room, or sing an innuendo-laden ghazal targeted at a blushing matron, but Aunty Bindu was out of his league. He would blush when he saw her, and when her pallav slipped to display those shy pale breasts, he would look away, always.

Once, when I was waiting at the Mallital rickshaw stand, in the queue for a cycle rickshaw to ferry me across to Tallital, I found Kaka Kohli standing behind me. He was searching for change—a ride across the Mall Road cost fifty paise in those days—when his wallet fell down, right by my feet. And there was her photograph staring out at me, the pretty pouting portrait Bindu had posed for at the Himalayan Studio, in the Burra Bazaar.

'Where did you get her picture?' I asked him. 'I mean, how?'

'God is Great,' he replied unhesitatingly, 'and your Aunty Bindu is blind not to see how much I love her. Don't tell her, please, that you saw her photograph in my wallet.'

Two rickshaws turned up, together, and I got into mine. As the rickshaw-wallah pedalled furiously down the road, his cycle bell chiming musically in time to the army quartet playing in the Bandstand, I worried. I had been drawn into a sort of complicity with Kaka Kohli, about his love and that photograph.

My father was in the army, and when he was posted to faraway Poona, we left Nainital to be with him. Then my father was posted to London for a while, as military attaché in the High Commission. My grandfather died, and our visits to Nainital became less and less frequent.

I remember arriving in Nainital with my mother in late August, two months before my first marriage. The receding monsoon had hit the lower Himalayas with manic fury. It was as though the whole town, nestled in the mountains, was a vaporous extension of the lake.

I had come with my mother to examine the jewellery stored in her bank locker, to see which of the 'sets' I wanted to appropriate. The heavy gold pahunchis and long matarmala, the traditional hansuli and the hand rafted chandrahar were lovely but I longed for something more modern. I tried to explain this to my mother but the conversation deteriorated into an acrimonious exchange.

We weren't talking to each other, my mother and I, when we saught refuge from the incessant rain in the Boathouse Club. My aunt Bindu was there, sitting on the covered verandah beside the deck, staring out at the lake. She was nursing a glass of Campa Cola; it was the year Coca-Cola had been banned from bottling in India. Something about her looked different, a sort of molecular reconstitution. I gave her a kiss, and realized from the small of her that it was a rum and coke that she was drinking.

Her pallav fell, and I observed that her neck and chest were afflicted with large spreading patches of leucoderma. She pulled it up wearily, no longer a playful cloud caressing the remote mountain peaks.

The rain cleared, and we left for home before the downpour began again. There was a smell of damp everywhere, and the rain rattled on the roof like a million clanking manual typewriters recording dictation at 180 w.p.m. I had just joined an advertising agency as a trainee, and I can remember congratulating myself on my clever metaphor. A bolt of lightning, a thunderclap, and the electric supply broke down. My mother found a torch and then some candles and, finally, a damp matchbox. We sat in the light of two spluttering candles while the wind whooshed through the broken windowpane, an impudent intruder.

We had made our peace by now, my mother and I. It had been agreed that we would reset her modest diamond earrings into a pair of danglers, in the very latest style. It was fun to sit with my mother and talk in whispers, undercutting the fury of the rain.

'What's happened to Aunty Bindu?' I asked. 'She looks so different, not at all like she used to . . .'

My mother's voice fell to a conspiratorial whisper, so I could hardly hear her over the battering raindrops. Things were not going well with Bindu. Her husband, Uncle Omit, had turned religious and joined the Hartaula

Ashram in Almora. He had taken premature retirement and retreated into a world of fasting, meditation and occasional, unpredictable vows of silence. The bank had been instructed to remit his pension into her account every month. Their son was in boarding school, in Sherwood College here in Nainital. The school fees were paid from Omit's savings. 'He is allowed to meet his mother only on one weekend every month,' my mother whispered. 'I wonder what went wrong with her life . . .'

The wind wrestled with the broken windowpane, and one of the candles collapsed into a mess of smoke and beeswax. I remembered how her pallav would fall off her shoulders, and how she would struggle to rearrange it into a demure, obedient drape. I wondered if uncle Omit had found that charming, if it had endeared her to him. Perhaps it hadn't. And I thought of my fiancé Pranesh, and a chill wind wandered in like a premonition to settle around my heart.

I've forgotten the sequence of events after that. I got married to Pranesh that October, and we lived in Canada for a year, where the size and scale of its lakes shocked and shamed me into reassessing my previous understanding of the word. Nainital was a faraway memory, its green waterbody a distant provincial pond.

We returned to Nainital one summer, when it was so crowded with tourists and honeymooners that I felt I had wandered into a waking nightmare. Every one of the tourists seemed to be carrying a transistor and each of the transistors seemed to be playing the same set of Hindi film tunes. The hills were echoing and reverberating with love songs, and here was Kaka Kohli adding to the din, humming and whistling the very latest hit songs.

His grey eyes lit up when he saw me, and he broke into a wide smile. His front tooth had gone missing, and he looked like a cover of *Mad* magazine. 'Remember,' he hissed, 'God is Great and Love Is Bloody Blind.'

That was the day Bindu walked into the lake and drowned. Or almost. Her sari spread out like a billowing yacht sail as she slid into the green waters from the jetty by the underdeck. Two boatmen saw her disappearing into the lake and dived in after her. Nainital Lake is very deep at that point, but they managed to pull her out somehow. Her feet had got tangled in the duckweed, but she was still breathing, although only just.

Kaka Kohli and all the others playing rummy in the card room had collected by the deck to watch the rescue, their mouths agape. The boatmen dragged her lifeless body out, and Kaka leapt upon her and began mouth-to-mouth resuscitation. Then a lady doctor arrived, and she punched and pummelled to get out the water in her lungs.

I wasn't there, but it was told to me, a blow-by-blow account, as it was to everyone in Nainital, including the tourists, who even turned off their transistors for a while to listen to the true-life tale of the lady who walked into the lake.

We went to visit her, in Ramsay Hospital, and she seemed vacant and confused. Her son Sunil had come to visit her, and he was sitting glumly by the door, looking distant and blank. Pranesh tried to talk to him, and then Kaka Kohli arrived, not smiling. He took out his wallet and opened it. There was the photo of Bindu, looking like a cross between Geeta Dutt and Helen, with a flower in her hair and a pretty pout on her lips.

'Look at this photograph, Binduji,' Kaka Kohli said hoarsely. 'For so many years, I have carried this photo. For so many years, I have loved you. Why? Why? Why? Because I am a prem pujari, a priest of love.

'I had a girlfriend in Lahore, when I was young. She was a Muslim girl, and she died during the Partition riots. My mother died too, and my sister. I wanted to die, but I returned to life. Because God is Great. Because Love is Blind. Don't do this to yourself, Binduji. Return to life.'

She had fallen asleep. Her eyes were shut, and her chest was heaving gently under the white hospital sheet. I took Sunil to the flats and bought him two bars of chocolate and a key ring that said IMAGINE in a psychedelic script. This cheered him up, and he seemed to be getting along with Pranesh.

'Who was that man who visited your aunt?' Pranesh asked me later, after we had deposited Sunil back at the hospital.

'Oh, he's just a man,' I explained. 'A Nainital local. He owns the Metropole Hotel, and I think maybe he was one of her admirers, when she was young . . .'

We left the next day, and returned to Canada soon after. Three months later, Bindu walked into the lake again, near the Pashan Devi temple. A student from the local Degree College saw her disappearing into the water, and raised an alarm. But her body had drifted into the rock crevices below the temple, and it was a month before the divers found her.

My mother wrote to tell me what had happened, and telephoned to fill in the details. I was so wounded at that stage by my own accelerating marital battles that I reacted with a dumb detachment: things happened to people. I wrote a suitable letter to her son Sunil, and decided sensibly that there was no point in writing to Uncle Omit.

It was all a long time ago, and probably of no consequence to anyone any more. But I had to record and remember this, to relive those days, and learn again from Kaka Kohli's obituary announcement the enduring message of his life.

If we break Kaka's dictum into two logical halves, the subtext is easier to process. 'God is Great' is a stratagem of outright surrender, allowing us to overlook fate, injustice and bad luck with the possibility of a palliative leave-it-to-the-manufacturer policy. And 'Love is Bloody Blind' resonates with all categories of emotional pain and malfunction.

Few humans are privileged to live a life measured and guided by a personal philosophy. Diogenes, the cynic of Greece, spent his years holding up a lantern in daylight searching for an honest man. Kaka, that unrecognized messiah, had crafted a more compassionate creed. GIGALIBB.

Hamsadhwani

Earth, sky, water. We swans know how to navigate them all. When we soar into the ether with outstretched wings, as we begin on our summer flight to the south, we view the world of humans from a different perspective. I see forests and rivers and sometimes farms, where the shadows of clouds reflect on the shallow water troughs of the paddy fields. Sometimes, flecks or shadows of humans can be seen, toiling up a mountain, fording a river, clustered in a market square.

I have always wondered about the human race. Confined to earth, they are less strong than elephants or tigers or even horses, and yet they have about them a will, a sense of self, that drives them in most inexplicable ways. Humans do not live life as we others do, they fight and resist the natural order of things. If you look at their cousins the monkeys you are struck by the similar ways in which they pick the nits out of their hair, and the way they pass their turds on to the earth. The yetis, noble creatures of the snow, of course, are very different, but it is humans who have always fascinated me.

Every year, for many generations now, our clan winters in the region of Vidarbha. Then, as the seasons change, we sojourn once again to the lakes of the Himal. Manasarovar mirrors Mount Kailash, the seat of Shiva. It was on this lake that I met my mate Hamso. We glimpsed each other reflected in the gathering waters of the lake, two egg-born ones paddling side by side under the blinding beauty of the snow-topped mountains. I had paused to shake off some weed entangling my feet. Hamso stopped too. I saw his gleaming golden wings in the mirror of Manasarovar's waters. The sun was reflected upon the rippling waves, lighting through the surface all the way to the bottom of the lake. I looked into the transparent waters of Manasarovar, and knew in that moment that my life was bound with his. Hamso. Soham. I was he. He, too, knew this. We fell into pace and navigated the lake together, one circle to the right and two to the left. When we reached the western shore of the lake, Hamso plucked a young lotus bud and placed it in my beak. Thus, we were betrothed and pledged to journey together all our days.

Swans are not like sparrows, who rub their feathers and

pleasure each other anytime, anywhere, with anyone of their species. No, we swans value loyalty and understand love. Flying with the clouds, over mountains and fields, forests and rivers, we can hear the Hamsadhwani, the twang of love's lyre, as it plays in human hearts.

What I shall tell you is a story about love, if not a love story. Saraswati, the goddess of speech and song, appointed me to tell this tale, since I had seen it, indeed, made it all happen. Once, when the yellow-robed goddess had chosen to ride me, she pointed the unfeathered skin between my eyes and bill to the palace in Vidarbha where Princess Damayanti sat dreamily on a low swing, in a bower of madhumalti blossoms. She looked as though she were waiting for all the stories in the world to unfold and play themselves out before her.

'Mark her,' the goddess Saraswati said to me. 'That maiden carries the sign of the half-moon on her brow. In another age, it is the future tale of Damayanti and her husband Nala that will instruct Yudhisthira, the most righteous man ever born, in how to conduct himself through misfortune.' She was talking of the devastating events that preceded the great war at Kurukshetra, but at that moment, in that time, Damayanti was simply a young human creature, sitting on a swing with the bees buzzing in and out of the flowering bushes to flirt with the tendrils of silky hair that framed her forehead.

Something of her remained with me—her radiant face and her pensive smile. That evening, when I met my mate Hamso at sundown, I told him of Princess Damayanti, and of the prophecy the goddess had uttered.

The next day, as we were returning northwards on our summer flight, we rested in the water gardens of Nala, king of the Nishadas. Hamso had known Nala for many seasons: every spring, every autumn, they would meet and renew their friendship. They talked of books, of philosophy, of life, Hamso sharing tales of our migration, the people we encountered and the lands we explored, and Nala telling him of how he steered his horse-drawn chariots, and how he longed someday to fly through the ether like my mate. Nala was a mortal with human constraints, but everything about him—his looks, his bearing, his character—had a whiff of the divine.

On that day, Nala had looked dreamy. 'I have seen her in my waking dreams, this lady whom I already love to distraction. I picture her in a garden, her handmaidens playing with the silken cords that pull her garlanded swing. She has the mark of the half-moon on her brow. She—she alone—will be my wife. But I do not know her name, or how to woo and win her!'

'Her name is Princess Damayanti,' I said in a whisper, 'and she is the daughter of Bhima, king of Vidarbha, to whom she was conferred as a boon. The story of your love will instruct many generations to come . . .' I remembered the words of the goddess, but clamped shut my mouth and pushed back the phrase. Tidings of love that began with misfortune? I would not say it, believe or remember it.

Hamso's eyes met mine, soft with sympathy. Nala was striding up and down the garden in a paroxysm of excitement. 'Go to her, Hamso, and tell her of my distraction, my infatuation, my madness. Now that I know her name, now that your lady has confirmed our fate, I cannot live another moment without her. Take my tidings of love to her.' He tore off his seven-string necklace of pearls and coral and iridescent lapis lazuli and flung it to Hamso. 'Take this to her, and bring back her heart to me!'

'Princess Damayanti's heart beats within her, King Nala, and yours within you,' my mate said, 'and yet they can be as one.' He looked at me, and I could feel the life in him coursing through me, and mine in him.

But this tale is not about me—Hamsahini—or Hamso. It is about Nala and Damayanti, and I must take the trouble to tell it. So, let me begin again.

*

Nala was the handsome and valorous king of the Nishadas. His kingdom lay in the high mountains, by the river Alaknanda. Nala was resplendent as the sun, and skilled beyond measure with horses and chariots. Damayanti, radiant sister of three noble brothers, had been conferred as a boon on King Bhima of Vidarbha, which lies beyond the Vindhyas. Nala and Damayanti were destined to be soulmates, and fell in love without ever meeting each other. A swan with golden wings was the emissary of their passion. This swan and his mate flew from Nala's palace to the pleasure grove in Vidarbha where Damayanti sat gossiping with her friends. She had flawless limbs, her body was a flash of lightning that disturbed the very gods. The swan addressed Damayanti in human tongue: 'O Damayanti, there is a king of the Nishadas by the name of Nala. I have seen gods, gandharvas, mortals, serpents and rakshasas, but none like him. I have brought a message from King Nala, and this seven-string necklace of pearls and coral and lapis lazuli, as a declaration of his passion. You were meant for Nala and none other, and he shall come to seek your hand in marriage.'

The princess seemed to know already that this was to be. She swooned with passion and gave her consent. The egg-born ones ascended the skies and flew on golden wings to tell Nala of Damayanti's love. Flapping his fair wings to fan the fire of the Nishada king's love, the swan told Nala of Damayanti, the daughter of Vidarbha, who carried the mark of the half-moon on her proud brow. They hadn't seen each other, but they knew, by the beating of the swan's wings, that their hearts were one, and their fates conjoined.

*

Perhaps motivated by the gossip from the women's palace, Bhima decided to hold a swayamavara for his daughter, so she might choose the man worthy to be her husband. All sorts of suitors—mortal and immortal—rushed to Vidarbha to seek Damayanti's hand in marriage. The gods were on their way, too, when they encountered Nala, speeding in his customized carriage towards Vidarbha, the message of the golden swan imprinted on his heart.

We too were there, flying overhead, returning to Vidarbha with Nala. Hamso had never before delayed the flight to the high mountains, never spent a summer anywhere except in the sacred Manasarovar. But the duties of friendship bound us to Nala now, even as late spring lingered on the fevered forehead of summer.

It was easy, in those times, to recognize the gods. Although the divinities had come on a human task—to win Damayanti's love—they were nevertheless immortals and to be respected as such. They sized him up, this handsome king, who had the desperation of extreme passion written in his every feature and directing his every movement. With their customary deviousness, the immortals first humbled Nala by asking him for a boon. Being a king and a warrior, he agreed. 'Do not pursue Princess Damayanti at her swayamvara,' they demanded, opportune humility giving way to a relieved arrogance. King or commoner, humans in those times generally respected the gods and so, the noble Nala conceded to their request.

I don't know where the difference between human and divine lusts lies. Perhaps, the hungers of the gods cast no shadows. Determined to vanquish the hopes and loves of a mere mortal, the gods played a further trick on Princess Damayanti, refracting and projecting their images into a hundred echoes and simulations so that she could not recognize Nala, king of the Nishadas, even as he stood before her. But the message of the swan fluttered in her heart. Without hesitation, she saw through the chimeras and garlanded Nala, the man to whom her fate and future were already wedded.

The gods saw this and were angered. The displeasure of the gods is often undeserved, but humans can seldom evade its consequences. Their destinies hang from improbable strings, pulled by unknown puppeteers.

*

King Nala returned with his wife, Queen Damayanti, to his mountain kingdom, where they pleasured like restless sparrows and rejoiced in the youthful joys of beauty, strength and desire. The king and his charioteer would drive the queen in the royal carriage to the high passes that led between steep cliffs and through deep ravines to the heart of the Himal, the Manasarovar, lake of the mind.

I have observed this about human nature: mortals tend not to value happiness when they have it. Taking no note of the changing seasons, they assume that the sum of joys will always grow and spread like a summer creeper.

An evil spirit, Kalee, harboured an animus against the noble and handsome Nala. The ghost of a much-hated demon, born of the midnight mating of a vampire and an incubus, misbegotten Kalee wandered through the mountain passes, searching for victims to contaminate with his evil tricks. Kalee hated Nala for the honour and happiness he enjoyed, and the joys he shared with Damayanti. Malefic Kalee came to the unsuspecting Nala as his fate, infecting him with dishonour.

By the mountain pass that leads to the plateaus of Tibet, there stands a tall deodar tree with a creeper of poison ivy growing like a cloud around it. This was the lair of Kalee, the spot where he meditated on hatred. As Nala's chariot thundered through the pass, Kalee curled himself into a ball, smaller than a caterpillar, and settled on a ripening leaf that floated down and settled on Nala's shoulder. Nala scratched his neck, and brushed the leaf off. But Kalee remained, perched on his shoulder, whispering gentle, seductive suggestions of self-destruction.

Determined to destroy Nala, cunning Kalee suggested to Nala's brother, the jealous Pushkar, through the whisper of hate, that he challenge the king of the Nishadas to a decisive game of dice. Like Yudhisthira after him, Nala succumbed to the provocation. The fever of chance, the joy of controlling the lying dice, overtook Nala in his mind and his heart. The square faces of the dice are marked as follows: Satya is signified with four dots; Trita with three; Dwapara with two; and Kali with one, illustrating the four yugas and the progressive decline of dharma through the ages. Victory lies in the fourth face of the dice, despair and defeat in the single dot of Kali.

The scornful gods enjoy sporting with the human race. How the dice fall is determind by the karma of the gambler. While the thrill of gambling had previously held no attraction for him, Nala was addicted to speed, to the wind in his ears as he raced against it in his chariot. It was in his nature, under his skin, a gambler's unawakened instinct.

Dice are crafted from vibhitika nuts. Lacquered with red and black, ornamented with gold insets, they are the sport of kings, the game of life. To resist the call of the dancing dice is to resist the challenge of living, or so the gambler thinks and feels. Nala watched, enraptured as they challenged all that was stable and auspicious. Falling on the diceboard they indicated always the sign of defeat, so positioned by the incubus Kalee.

Late that autumn, Hamso and I saw the pleasure gardens of the Nishada palace low under the clouds. King Nala was squatting on a silk and hessian mat, surrounded by cushions and bolsters, playing at dice with his jealous brother Pushkar. His hair in uncharacteristic disarray, his face distraught, Nala's eyes were darting this way and that. The radiant Damayanti was not by his side.

The last rays of the setting sun touched Hamso's wings, a shining span of gleaming feathers and golden sunlight. 'We shall not stop to meet our friend this day,' Hamso said pensively. 'Gambling is based not on luck but on probability; it is the domain of the mathematical mind, not of an impetuous warrior. It is not to do with chance or luck, but with patterns seen and unseen. I fear Nala has fallen prey, become the sport of the jealous gods.'

The handsome king of the Nishadas thought fortune a matter of valour. For days and months, he gambled with his brother Pushkar, refusing no challenge. He lost first himself, then his treasury of gold, then his chariots, their golden yokes, and even his garments. His ministers, advisers and the prominent citizens of the realm, all urged him to stop, but the spirit of self-destruction had overtaken Nala.

*

And so it continued, with Nala losing all that he possessed except his wife Damayanti. Together they left the city gates, through the thorny underbrush that led to the forest, to travel the path of self-exile. No longer favoured by fortune, Nala, king of the Nishadas, had been rendered powerless by the throw of the dice. Dishonoured by his ministers, receiving no homage from his subjects, he slept under the stars, stripped of royalty and radiance.

Tired, thirsty and dispirited, Nala observed a flock of celestial-looking birds descend from the sky. They hovered around him and his queen, whose radiance had not abandoned her. The birds, it seemed, had plumage of the purest gold. Because of his friendship with us, the hapless Nala trusted them, believed them to be auspicious. But they were not of the race of royal swans—mere chimeras, they were creatures of deceit. Kalee, that spirit of misfortune who still nestled determinedly in Nala's heart, spoke to him from the blood that coursed through his veins.

'Surely I can win back my riches, reverse the throw of those fatal dice.' With that thought, Nala flung his sole garment over the birds, certain he could trap them. The golden birds twittered in unison and flew off into the sky, leaving Nala stripped of human shame, naked under the sky.

'We are the playful dice,' the golden birds sang as they flew off into the sky. 'We are the emblems of your misfortune.' Regal Damayanti shared her single garment with her husband, and together they wandered the forests, seeking refuge from their tormenting memories of happiness.

Naked, hungry and despairing, Nala urged his loyal wife to leave him and return to her father Bhima and the comforts of the palace. Finally, unable to persuade her, he abandoned her, relinquishing Damayanti to her fate as he wandered up hill and down dale, through forest paths that led nowhere.

Damayanti searched for her beloved Nala. Stumbling barefoot through the dense forest, she was left untroubled by the lurking bhootas and pisachas, but was nurtured by the spirits of the trees, and vanbhanjikas. She ate nettles, and sometimes berries, and thorns encircled the soft feet that had once been adorned with gold anklets. The blessings of the hermits whom she met in her wanderings led her to a caravan travelling to Chedi.

Yet the relentless shadow of misfortune followed her. One night, as the tired travellers rested under the stars, a herd of wild tuskers wandered into their camp and trampled upon them as they slept. The frightened horses fled this way and that, maiming and killing those who had escaped the wild elephants. Only the ill-fated Damayanti survived. Nala's wife observed the destruction around her, and grieved and lamented at having spread the contagion of her ill luck to those who had kindly sheltered her.

I am losing track of the story, getting lost in the narrative. Where was Nala, cursed king of the Nishadas, as his unfortunate wife suffered the consequences of his actions?

Nala was in another part of the forest, not far from where Damayanti sat weeping as she surveyed the corpses of her fellow-travellers. The great beasts of the forest wait to devour the dead, but even they kept away; they would not attack Damayanti, whose living fate was worse than death.

Nala was clutching the portion of the garment he had torn off Damayanti's sleeping body when he saw a great orange light before him, dancing through the forest like a maddened elephant. It was a forest fire, crackling and laughing and devouring all it encountered. The disgraced king glimpsed the chance of salvation and rushed wildly into the flames, embracing them with the desperate love he had once reserved for Damayanti.

As he stepped in, Nala heard a voice rise through the whooshing of the flames. 'Save me, O king!' The voice entreated, 'Save me, valorous Nala!'

Karkotaka, king of the snakes, lay coiled at the centre of the trembling fire. 'I have been cursed by a brahmarishi to this fate. Rescue me and I shall be your friend in redressing your fortunes.'

We swans know the inner minds of snakes, for we are descended from the union of Garuda and Naga, eagle and serpent—from the union and balance of opposites. The honour of snakes runs as deep as their pride.

Hearing Karkotaka's appeal, the disgraced king of the Nishadas advanced into the heart of the fire to save the snake. With the magic of the Naga race, Karkotaka willed his enormous coils to become as light as a bundle of dried leaves. Nala, weak and emaciated though he was, picked him up and escaped the fire's fury. His hair was singed, his skin marked by burns, but Nala was happy that his misfortunes had not prevented him from the dharma of a warrior, and that he had been able to save the life of one who sought his protection.

Karkotaka addressed Nala: 'Measure your steps, King Nala, as you walk. When you tread the count of ten, halt for a moment.' At the tenth step, Karkotaka swung forward and stung his saviour with his forked golden tongue. Nala could feel the sharp wound as the poison coursed through him like an intoxication. He saw his arms shrivel and shrink; his tall frame scrunched into that of a deformed hunchback. The king of the snakes, who had envenomed him, stood transformed, now bearing the tall body that had once been Nala's.

'I am your grateful well-wisher, Nala, and there is good reason for my action. This venom in your body is aimed at the incubus who has entered you. The evil spirit Kalee, who is perverting your fate and judgement, will have to suffer this poison as long as he hides within your form.'

Metamorphosis has its complications. Having entered Nala, the animus that Kalee harboured against the once-fortunate king was beginning to feed on itself. The spirit of misfortune heard Karkotaka's words and grimaced.

He would not be so easily exorcised, resolved Kalee; but somewhere, the revenge on Nala was beginning to turn sour.

'Your body is safe in my power of illusion. The contours of flesh, bone and tissue shall remain intact, contained from the poison I have injected in your veins. Direct yourself to Rituparna, the king of Ayodhya. Offer your services as the chief groom of his horses. He shall teach you the secret of the dice. When this verminous goblin within you repents and leaves your shade, cast this garment over you and think of me. Your body shall then be returned to you, strong and lustrous as ever before.'

King Nala, dispossessed now of even his body, followed the serpent's instructions and joined the stables of Rituparna of Ayodhya as a groom. His startling accomplishments as a charioteer soon won him the affection and trust of the king. Nala would whisper to the horses about lost love and human folly, and his tears fell on the hay as the rearing stallions consoled him with the gentlest of neighs.

*

Damayanti's luck began to take a turn for the better. As she sat grieving in the forest, a merchant named Shuchi emerged from the bower of creepers, where he and some others had hidden from the marauding tuskers. Moved by her sorrow, Shuchi took Damayanti back with him in the depleted convoy that returned to the kingdom of Chedi. The kind-hearted merchant left her in the marketplace, to find her way in the city. There, the queen mother spotted her and took Damayanti into her household.

Coincidence—the conjoining of fate and events—is but the confirmation of destined paths. In Chedi, the king's mother, who had so generously sheltered Damayanti in her palace, felt inexplicably drawn to the silent and enigmatic lady. Examining her oddly familiar face, she saw a mark shaped like a half-moon and covered by dirt, on the brow of her newly-employed handmaiden.

'How did you get that mark on your brow?' she asked.

'At birth,' Damayanti replied. 'It is a sign of my moon-born lineage.'

The queen mother's heart leapt into her mouth. This was, she realized, none other than her niece, the daughter of her sister, who was married to Bhima of Vidarbha.

The king of Chedi was informed of this strange turn of events, and he made arrangements to have his new-found cousin returned with full royal honour to her father's palace.

I will not describe the happiness of aunt and mother, of Damayanti's noble brothers, of the celebrations that King Bhima ordered in honour of his daughter's return. Only Damayanti did not stop to rejoice. On reaching her father Bhima's palace, she began to search afresh for her missing husband. For the sake of his daughter, King Bhima dispatched his most astute brahmin spies in all eight directions to search for Nala.

'Tormented by grief, distracted by your memory, your wife is awaiting you, still clad in only half a garment, as you had left her in the forest. Why have you forgotten your loving wife?' This was the cry the king's spies were instructed to repeat, in every town square, at every crossroads, as they searched for Damayanti's husband Nala.

The travelling brahmins did as they had been instructed. On reaching the kingdom of Ayodhya, they declaimed these words at every market square and intersection, and wherever else they could. A diligent Brahmin spy observed that the deformed charioteer grooming the horses in the royal stables responded to this message by bursting into tears. He duly reported it to Damayanti who, once again, sensed the presence of her love from the words of a messenger.

Being as wise as she was constant, Damayanti devised a clever ruse. She sent the spy back to Ayodhya, to publicly announce that the abandoned wife of Nala king of the Nishadas, was holding another swayamvara, to choose a new husband.

King Rituparna and his hunchbacked charioteer, the metamorphosed Nala, rushed together to Vidarbha on wings of fire—Rituparna eager to claim Damayanti, Nala determined to prevent it. As they thundered down to Vidarbha, the hurtling chariot swallowing the vanishing yojanas, Rituparna said to his charioteer, 'Teach me the secrets of speed, the art of controlling horses, and I shall show you the inner life of numbers.'

'I shall do as you instruct, Your Majesty,' his deformed charioteer replied humbly.

'Halt and observe this vibhitika tree, crowded with fruit. In those two branches alone, this tree has five crore and five leaves. The fruits in those two branches number two thousand and ninety-five. The number of leaves and fruits that are on the tree is greater by one hundred and one than those that have fallen down . . .'

On the king's instructions, Nala stopped and cut down the tree and counted the fruits on the two branches. They numbered two thousand and ninety-five.

'I know the heart of the dice, and the inner secrets of counting,' Rituparna continued. 'The combined sums of the four faces of the dice do not lie in luck or divination, but the certainty of mathematics. Add and multiply possibilities, sense the flow of numbers, understand the nature of the probable. The secret of the dice lies not in will, but in understanding. The hidden face of fate and of the universe can be wrested only by the discipline and rigour of inquiry.'

This is perhaps what he said, though it is nowhere recorded in quite those words. And so, Nala learnt the secrets of equilibrium, of the balance of opposites. He learnt the value of living not by emotion or courage or sentiment, but by the unforgiving logic of reason and the mastery of the numbers that control it.

*

When they reached Vidarbha, King Rituparna rushed towards the beautiful Damayanti, seeking the garland of union that would make them one. But she had seen a hunchback with a misshapen arm, standing by the king's chariot, and her heart was engulfed by joy. To the astonishment of all around, she garlanded the deformed charioteer and held him to her breast. Damayanti was reunited with her lover.

The time had come. Following the instructions of Karkotaka, Nala spread, over his hunched back, the garment which the serpent had given him. Before the eyes of the astonished gathering, he sloughed off that misshapen body and assumed his own, strong and lustrous as ever. Nala and Damayanti returned to the kingdom of the Nishadas and challenged his brother Pushkar to a final game of dice. Now an adept in the art of counting, he also knew, after life's hard lessons, when to stop. Nala had understood how to change his luck with mathematics—that reliable and unforgiving branch of magic. That was how his friend, my mate Hamso, explained it to me.

*

That was the year winter set in early. The swanlings had departed, and it was past the time for us to return south, to follow the currents of the earth and the sky to the plains beyond Vindhyavasini. Hamso was silent and pensive, and I would see him fly off the lake to the further shore, his soaring wings like a prayer to the skies. They say the flight of the swan symbolizes the escape from the cycles of samsara.

The frost had wilted the lotus buds that grew by the northern shore of Manasarovar. The frozen surface of the lake was a mirror of blinding silver light, reflecting the eternal snows of Kailash. My mate lay very still on the sheet of ice.

'Hamso,' I whispered, but there was no reply. 'Hamso, Hamso . . .'

He had frozen to death. The life breath had left him, he had become a paramhamsa.

Hamso. I, Hamsahika, am that. Soham.

*

I think again of love, and of Nala and Damayanti, and the wayward fancies of the human race. This tale—that the goddess Saraswati instructed me to share—was recounted in the Mahabharata to Yudhisthira, to give him hope, and to help him snap out of self-pity. Like Nala, the king of the Nishadas, the Pandava had lost his kingdom and his noble queen in a skewed game of dice. The story is thus an inspiration for all who have tasted defeat and failure, and have had to win and validate their love anew. The swans that fly south from Manasarovar in the winters still cross the mountain peak named after Karkotaka, king of the snakes. It stands guard over the Nala Damayanti lake in Nainital. Love, misfortune and separation still haunt the honeymooners who come to the resorts and spa hotels there, drawn by the songs of fluttering swans. It may seem as though this happened a long time ago, but human folly hasn't changed, and neither have the unbending laws of mathematics and the inscrutable ways of the universe.

Omens II

I was in the Secrete Beauty Parlour, in the by-lanes of Old Baneswor. A young girl with fragrant fruity breath and armpits that smelt of damp monsoon laundry was dexterously threading the stubborn hairs on my chin. Her face was alarmingly close to mine: her eyes intent with concentration, her upper lip beaded with perspiration.

She gave me a sympathetic smile as she finished. 'It's hard work being a woman,' she concluded, dusting my now-smooth chin with Chinese talcum powder. She said 'woomun', not woman. I smiled back in solidarity.

Kathmandu had changed in the ten years since I had last been there. It seemed hotter, more crowded, but also, inexplicably, more itself. The Kathmandu valley is shaped like a gracious bowl, surrounded by mountains and clouds and invisible snow peaks. The Bagmati river threads its way through the valley, descending from Gokarna and making its way through muck, litter, debris and refuse towards the Terai, and then Bihar. I was attending a conference on migration, livelihood, and macro and micro identities. Most of the delegates were old Nepal hands; they loved the city and its environs. They talked of Pokhara and buff steaks and the Maoist paradigm, all with easy affection and familiarity. I left this jolly group of friends drinking beer and making PowerPoint presentations. I had promised my mother that I would go to the Pashupatinath temple to offer my prayers and seek the lord's blessings. They were meant to grant me a handsome, virile and solvent husband, and ease my mother's fears about my chronic spinsterhood. After expressing my solidarity with womanhood at the beauty parlour, I made my way there.

The golden gopuras of the temple glistened in the late afternoon light. Dark clouds alternated with startlingly bright rain-washed sunshine. Cows lowed and mooed in the cowsheds leading to the main temple. Suddenly, six armed guards in camouflage gear shooed me to the side of the narrow lane. They were marching behind a short straight-backed priest with a military bearing, dressed in saffron renunciant's robes, escorting him to the carved wooden rear entrance of the main Pashupati temple. He turned back for a moment, to instruct the guards about something. His eyes met mine. They were contemptuous, acid with scorn. I turned my gaze away and continued walking to the shrines that fronted the river. A portly matron, a Madras mami with an authentic trans-Tamil American accent crossed the bridge and began walking alongside me. She was escorting a young Australian girl, whom she was loudly instructing in the mystic ways of Hinduism. Her vowels and consonants were tumbling out in an unpredictable north-south sequence. 'This temple was built in 400 AD, thousands of years ago . . .'

'Wow!' her companion responded. 'I mean wow!'

The loquacious lady was wearing a denim one-piece catsuit and a Brahmin caste mark. Her feet were clothed in fuzzy airline socks and geisha-style rubber flip-flop slippers. Her face was framed in a halo of frizzy grey hair. Everything about her was both comic and grotesque, with an edge of the manic and the menacing in her loud voice and determined chatter. She ruined the experience of the temple for me, dispelling the romance and mood of timelessness.

'Non-Hindus are not allowed to enter the main temple, they can only come until here!' She continued, 'otherwise the curse of the termites will destroy the holy carvings.'

'Wow!' the Australian girl replied, the enthusiasm an octave lower.

I had come to pray to Shiva, the creator and destroyer of the universe. Not to hear these women's banalities. I walked on along the river, determined to leave them behind. There were no temples there, only some cave-like perches along the low cliffs bordering the Bagmati. A boy sat on one of them, playing on a wooden flute. Four black Bhutia dogs clustered around him, flapping their ears in appreciation. The sound of the flute was like a musical sorbet after the Chennai amma's chatter. I walked up, following the music.

The boy was perched on a makeshift wooden platform, like a deck, protruding from a narrow slit in the rock. He summoned me up, and I followed him silently into the dark and spacious cave. It had a raised platform with a mattress on it. A body lay sprawled across the mattress, staring up at the ceiling.

'Hi!' a man's voice exclaimed, somehow picking up the accent and intonation of the Australian maiden whose 'wows!' I had just escaped. 'Welcome to my cave. I am a New Zealander who has entered the spirit of the guru who used to live in this space. I had a stroke four years ago, and they brought me here. I've been staring at the ceiling ever since. Would you like my blessings?'

Who were 'they', I wondered. Who had brought him here?

'The world may think I'm crazy but I'm not. The secrets of the universe become clear if you stare at the ceiling for a long time. And if you hear the sound of the river.'

I could hear the sound of the river, rushing below us, and the distant temple bells groaning and tinkling and chiming.

'Who are you?' I asked. 'Can I help you in any way?'

'I'm Tom,' the man replied. 'I'm all right. The guru is watching over me, helping me to rise above the ceiling. My right arm is paralysed, and my leg too. But I manage. My spirit is intact.'

I fled the cave, dogged by fear and pity.

'Don't go,' Tom said. 'Don't go away, please. I haven't talked to anybody in English for a very long time.'

I left.

The damp pungent smoke from a funeral pyre filled the air. The body was piled with wood and grass, but the fire refused to catch. An exasperated-looking priest was rearranging the logs, trying to fan the flames. There were no relatives around to mourn, at least none that I could see.

The dead man's feet were uncovered, they looked incredibly fragile and mortal as they peered out from under the heap of wood and grass. Pale yellow in colour, they were covered with mud and dirt. The feet of a man who was used to walking barefoot, trekking through hills and woods.

A beam of light broke through the clouds and lit up his toes. They looked translucent, as though they belonged to some liminal plane between the dead and the living.

Perhaps the scalp had finally come alight, for I could smell hair burning. The stench made me retch, and I retreated from the temple, all religiosity forgotten.

In the sky, the clouds were scattering again, and a weak rainbow arched across the valley: a blessing, a consolation.

Author's Note

These stories were written, on and off, over several years. They have been imagined in airports, scribbled during flights, corrected in traffic jams, deciphered from the backs of envelopes. Be it ancient myth or modern malaise, the narrative voices seem to carry an imprint of anxiety and resignation. They are meant neither to amuse nor to instruct, but if the reader flips through them and nods in occasional sympathy, their tale is told.

Acknowledgements

My thanks to Sivapriya, and all at Penguin, for their constant support.